MY DIRTY DUKE

JOANNA SHUPE

Cover Design: Letitia Hasser, RBA Designs

Editing: Sabrina Darby

Proofing: Dee Hudson and Michelle Li at Tessera Editorial

MY DIRTY DUKE

JOANNA SHUPE

CHAPTER 1

*J*t was the social event of the year and Violet was squandering it. She should have been dancing or chatting with friends. Instead, she was propped against the wall, hiding in plain sight, staring at him.

She could not stop staring at him.

The ballroom was filled with titled lords and ladies, but she was always able to find him. He was tall, nearly the tallest man in any room. Elegantly dressed. Starkly handsome, without frills to pretty up his visage. His features were strong, harsh like a Roman warrior, with dark hair, and eyes like twin pools of midnight. If she could photograph him right now, the caption would read, "Feared by most, revered by the rest."

Once upon a time he spoke to her with kind words, during her parents' dinner parties when she was deemed old enough to attend. That was before finishing school. Before her debut. Violet fell in love with him then, this intelligent and beautiful man who commanded every room.

At the time, she hadn't a clue as to why her stomach dipped and swirled in his presence. Now, at eighteen, she understood. She'd read books and seen racy photographs. Moreover, she'd overheard the maids talking about their beaus. So, Violet knew why her breathing quickened around him, knew the reason for the slickness between her thighs when she thought about being alone with him. Why she possessed this mad desire to have him smile at her again.

He never looked at her, though. Not once. Nor did he visit her father, his closest friend, at their home any longer. Since Violet's debut, he'd not asked her to dance, though most of her father's friends had indulged her at least once. He hadn't even spoken to her during her season. It was as if she were beneath his notice.

But then, most of London was beneath him. He was a duke.

And not merely any duke. His was one of the wealthiest and oldest of the titled families, the Duke of Ravensthorpe, Maximilian Thomas William Bradley III. She once looked his lineage up in Debrett's and learned that the very first Ravensthorpe received the title after thwarting an assassination attempt against Charles II.

"Why are you not dancing?" Her friend Charlotte appeared, her gaze studying Violet's face. "You are forever on the outskirts, observing. You should be having fun."

"I am taking a break."

"Who were you watching?" Charlotte's head swung about, searching. "Was it that newly widowed viscount everyone is talking about? He is scrumptious—and under thirty years of age."

"There is a newly widowed viscount?"

"Have you not heard? Honestly, Violet. What do you do with your time at these things?"

Stare at Ravensthorpe, obviously. "Why should I exert myself to learn all the latest gossip when I have you to do that for me?"

Charlotte laughed. "Fair enough. Tell me, at whom are you staring? Perhaps I can help you get his attention."

"Do not be silly. There is no one here for me. Just a bunch of old dukes and boring dandies."

"The dandies are quite nice to look at, however. Better than the stodgy dukes."

Not all dukes are stodgy, Violet wanted to say. Some were quite glorious.

"I wish I had my camera," she told her friend. "Then I could prove to you how not boring it is to watch."

Her father had gifted her with a camera two years ago and Violet had been taking photographs ever since. She'd converted a space in their attic into a developing room and had been studying photography at London Polytechnic for the last six months. She liked the challenge of photography, of achieving the perfect image. One of her dreams was to someday photograph Ravensthorpe, to capture the harsh angles and pretty features of his face. The cool stare and the haughty lift of his brow. Then she could have the image forever.

Such was the advantage of photographs. They were a way to record an instant, preserve a memory that might otherwise have been forgotten to the sands of time. Who knew what sorts of discoveries were ahead as cameras grew more advanced?

Violet continued to watch Ravensthorpe out of the corner of her eye so as not to alarm Charlotte. Her friend would try to dissuade Violet from her singular purpose this season, which was to somehow get Ravensthorpe to notice her. Again.

Suddenly, a woman walked behind Ravensthorpe and lightly touched his shoulder. The edge of the duke's mouth hitched and he leaned to whisper in the woman's ear. She was a countess, wife to the Earl of Underhill. Whatever the duke said must have satisfied her because she nodded once, and then slipped through the terrace doors.

An assignation?

Envy spiked in Violet's blood, violent and sharp, like she had poked herself with an embroidery needle. Charlotte kept talking, not taking notice of Violet's discomfort, and Violet was glad for it. She needed to gain control over her emotions.

Perhaps Ravensthorpe would not go. He would reconsider and decide—

Her stomach sank as he excused himself and followed the countess out the terrace doors. Definitely an assignation. She could hardly catch her breath; jealousy lodged in her lungs. She longed to beckon him to the gardens where she could touch and kiss him, explore that generous mouth and bask in his stern gaze . . .

Violet fanned herself vigorously as she burned with curiosity. What would Ravensthorpe and the countess do in the gardens, kiss? Fellatio? Sexual congress?

There was so much more she needed to know. For example, was Ravensthorpe a bold and demanding lover? Selfish? Or was he eager to please, as many of the erotic photographs she'd seen depicted? Perhaps if she learned more about what he liked, then she stood a better chance of getting him to notice her.

Charlotte must have perceived that Violet's attention had wandered. "Violet? One minute you are flushed and the next, pale as flour. What is wrong with you?"

She had to go. She had to see what was about to happen in the gardens. There wasn't a moment to lose.

Gripping Charlotte's arm, she kissed her friend's cheek. "I apologize. I'm not feeling well. I think I shall tell my father I'd like to go home."

Charlotte nodded, her expression brimming with affection and concern. "Excellent idea. Go on, then. Rest. I'll call on you tomorrow."

Violet bid Charlotte good night, then wove through the crowd, pretending to search for her father. In reality, her goal was to lose Charlotte and blend into the crush. With a final check to ensure no one was watching, she slipped through the French doors and onto the terrace.

The night smelled of lilacs and fresh dirt. Only a sliver of moon added to the soft torchlight along the edge of the garden path. Lifting her skirts, she moved carefully, desperate to not make any noise. She had been to this house before and knew the garden was designed as a large square, with a fountain at the far end. Tall hedges surrounded the path, high enough to offer cover to any couple. Her guess was that Ravensthorpe and the countess would meet near the fountain, farthest from the house.

She found a break in the bushes large enough to slip through and continued along the outside of the hedges bordering the lawn. Likely her slippers were ruined but she could not stop, not when she was close to discovering more about the duke. Sartorial sacrifices were necessary in the pursuit of all things Ravensthorpe.

Silent, she made her way along, allowing the hedge to be her guide in the dark. Near the final corner, she heard a lady's light laughter and a deep chuckle.

Ravensthorpe.

She crept closer, hardly daring to breathe. She needed to hear and see it all, so she bent and peered through the branches. After some maneuvering, she finally located the perfect vantage spot. Two figures were locked in an embrace, one of them clearly the duke.

Light from the house provided enough illumination to see that Ravensthorpe was kissing the countess, her body pressed tightly to his long frame. He clutched her waist with one hand while his other hand massaged her clothed breast. Violet's own nipples stiffened to peaks under her corset, the crisp air a delicious torture on her hot skin. The couple was ravenous, their mouths attacking one another between gasps of air.

In a flash, Ravensthorpe spun the countess so her back rested against his front, with both of them now facing Violet. He wrapped one set of his long fingers around the woman's throat as he shoved his other hand into her bodice. He lifted her breast out of her dress and undergarments, exposing it before caressing the plump flesh. His mouth slid along her cheek as the countess's lids fell shut, her lips parted with her rapid breathing.

"Look at you," he said, his voice like smooth silk. "A dirty girl with your gorgeous tit out. Ask me nicely and maybe I'll play with you."

"Please, Ravensthorpe," the countess whispered on a groan. "Oh, please."

Violet swallowed, her throat clogged with desire. Could they hear her heart pounding inside her chest? She would give anything to trade places with the older woman. Had the countess any idea of her good fortune?

"How pretty you are when you beg, Louisa."

Using the pads of his fingers, he stroked the taut bud at the tip of the countess's breast, pulling and pinching it. Louisa writhed, rubbing her body along his as he continued to work her, his other hand never leaving her throat.

Blood pooled between Violet's legs, her quim pulsing in time with her heartbeat. He was beautiful and compelling, an angel of sin and lust. Light reflected off the threads of silver at his temples, the effect like a match to her insides. She had never wanted anything or anyone more in all her eighteen years.

"If I lift your skirts, will I find you wet?" he asked.

Yes, Violet wanted to answer. *So very wet.*

The countess panted. "Oh, God. You . . ."

"Yes?"

"I cannot think. Please, do not stop."

"Do you need my cock, Louisa? Shall I place you over the end of that bench there and fuck you?"

Violet pressed her thighs together to ease her aching flesh. Sweet mother of mercy, he was potent. The angles of his face were harsh and unforgiving, his mouth almost cruel in its lasciviousness. Again she longed for her camera, wishing she could capture him in this stolen moment.

The countess shuddered at his words. "I cannot. As much as I crave you, I must return."

"What is another moment when I can make you come so hard?"

"Oh, you devil." She drew in a deep breath and covered his hand to stop his movements. "Unfortunately, I need to get back. I've been away too long. My husband will be wondering where I've gone."

"Hmm." Shifting her clothing, he tucked her breast away. Then he released her. "I suppose we will need to pick this up later, then."

The countess turned and bit his jaw, then drew her fingertip along the heavy ridge in his trousers. Ravensthorpe sucked in a breath, and she smiled. "Tonight, Ravensthorpe. Leave your side door unlatched. We'll play one of our naughty games."

Without waiting for his agreement, the countess hurried along the path toward the house. Ravensthorpe stood unmoving for a long moment, his chest rising and lowering in his evening clothes. A lock of dark hair had fallen over his forehead, a stripe of ink slashing his perfect skin. Violet could not look away, completely entranced.

He finally raised his head—only to pin her with a dark stare. "You may come out now, little mouse."

* * *

Violet froze.

Little mouse?

Was he talking to her? She had been so quiet, completely concealed by the hedges. Heavens, she was standing on the lawn. He couldn't possibly know she was there.

Cold terror filled her lungs as he walked directly toward her. She considered running, but where would she go? He'd see her for certain the instant she took off.

Bending, he came eye to eye with her from the other side of the hedge. "Come out of there, Violet. Now."

8

The tone was decidedly ducal, one used to being obeyed, and dread and embarrassment washed over her entire body. Violet prayed for the ground to open up and swallow her whole. She'd wanted him to notice her, but not like this. Never like this. She'd only wished to watch him with the countess like a voyeur hidden in the dark.

The hedges parted thanks to Ravensthorpe's arm, and there was soon enough room for her to slip through the branches. She tugged her skirts free, no doubt ripping the delicate silk. Clothing, however, was the least of her concerns.

Ravensthorpe's eyes were like frozen ice, a winter storm that chilled her to the bone. He put some distance between them, and his mouth was set in a flat, unhappy line when he whirled around. "What in hell do you think you are playing at?"

Her mind blanked in the face of his anger. "I went out for a walk."

"A lie. No lady walks on the lawn and risks her slippers." He pointed to her now-ruined footwear. "Again, what are you doing here?"

What happened if she admitted the truth? Would he finally see her as an adult, not some silly child he'd ignored for the past two years? She hated that he no longer talked to her. He acted as if she didn't exist, instead spending time with women who were married to other men, like the countess. What was so wrong with Violet?

"You are trying my patience, little mouse."

The truth fell from her lips. "I followed you."

"That is obvious," he said, the words like icicles, sharp and brittle. "What I cannot fathom is why."

"I was curious as to the type of woman who attracted you." She winced, but there was no taking it back now.

"Again, why?"

God above, was it not obvious? Was he actually going to make her speak it aloud?

You have nothing to lose. You have already embarrassed yourself.

"Because I wished to take her place, Your Grace."

Ravensthorpe dragged a hand down his face. Turning, he went to the iron bench near the fountain and sat, his long legs spread out before him. Violet wrapped her arms around herself, feeling like the world's biggest fool.

"Violet, you must return to the house and forget this ever happened.

You must forget *me*. There are dozens of men in there tonight who would gladly share a tryst with you."

"But they are not you," she whispered.

He winced as if struck. "I am far too old for you."

Old? She paused, blinking at him. He was not old. He was male perfection wrapped in a cloak of confidence and swagger. She'd seen plenty of decrepit men and Ravensthorpe was far from that group. Besides, it was nothing for a lord his age to wed a debutante. Such matches happened every season. "You are forty-one. Hardly old."

"No, but I am too old *for you*. I am your father's friend. I've known you since you were born, for God's sake."

"You are two years younger than my father, if memory serves."

He gave a dry laugh. "Christ, Violet. Are you trying to say two years makes a difference?"

"I don't care how old you are." There. She'd said it.

"You should. It would be far better for you to find a man your own age. Or close to it."

She cared little for the men her age. Foppish fools who worried more about appearances than anything else. During dances, they merely stared at her bosom and stepped on her toes.

Besides, how could she ever be interested in anyone other than Ravensthorpe? He'd starred in her dreams for so long there wasn't room for anyone else in her head. "I don't want a man my age." *I want you.*

"You are eighteen. You have a lifetime ahead of you. Find someone to share that life with, someone who makes you happy."

He appeared less angry at the moment and more like the kind man she remembered, so she decided to present him with a reasonable argument. "Many girls my age marry older men. It's common amongst the ton."

"Are you . . . Is this about becoming a duchess?" He sounded horrified. "Even if we were closer in age, I am not interested in marriage, ever. I will never take another wife."

She hadn't known his feelings on marriage, but she didn't care about titles. She wanted the man, end of story. If that was outside of marriage, so be it. "I am not proposing marriage, Your Grace."

"Christ, do not use my honorific in that tone of voice."

Why? She'd called him "Your Grace" hundreds of times. "I apologize, duke." It was a more personal form of address, one he would reserve for intimate members of his circle. She hoped to one day join that inner circle, whispering in his ear whilst they were in bed.

"Fuck, that is worse." Standing, he put his hands on his hips, an imposing tower of disapproval. Something about his scowl made her want to bow and scrape for his admiration. She nearly licked her lips. He said, "You are the daughter of my closest friend. This is inappropriate and needs to end, Violet."

She would not back down, not without answers. "Is that why you stopped talking to me? Why you won't even look at me anymore?"

He glanced away, not meeting her eyes. "I have no idea what you are talking about. I do not interact with children."

"You did. With me. For years and years. And then you stopped like I'd contracted smallpox."

"That was before. When it was harmless."

"What does that mean? Have I hurt you in some manner?" She didn't understand. He was speaking in riddles. She had made her position clear, yet could he not do the same?

A muscle jumped in his jaw. "Before you developed breasts and hips. Not to mention an arse I'd like to sink my teeth into. Have you no looking glass? Your body is made for sin and your face would make angels weep." He dragged a hand through his hair. "You have every man panting after you the second you walk into a bloody room."

Violet's knees wobbled. The air left her lungs and she feared she might faint. This was what Ravensthorpe thought of her? Lord above. She was rounder than most girls her age, with their tiny waists and bosoms that barely peeked out from their gowns. Indeed, she was what her mother called "robust."

But Ravensthorpe liked the way she looked. He said she had every man panting when she walked into a room. Did that mean him as well?

Was this why he no longer talked to her?

Men were so confusing.

"I don't understand," she said. "If you like the way I look, then why ignore me?"

Something dangerous flashed in his gaze. "You must stay away from me, Violet."

"Why? I am not pressuring you for marriage. I merely want . . ."

Heavy, angry footsteps brought him directly in front of her. "To fuck me. Is that it, little mouse? Do you need me to put my cock inside you and make you scream?"

Lust rushed through her veins, heavy and thick, and her lips parted as she exhaled. Lord, she wanted that so badly. To experience all she'd seen in those erotic photographs with the man standing in front of her.

He read the answer on her face. "Have you ever been fucked, Violet? Had a man's fingers inside your tight pussy? Or maybe a thick cock?" When she said nothing, he barked, "Answer me."

"No." She hadn't considered even trying with anyone other than the man standing in front of her.

"Do you even know what it's like to make yourself come? Do you stroke your clitoris under the covers at night, or perhaps in the bath?"

Her mouth dried out, speech impossible. Triumph lit his eyes, as if he'd succeeded in exposing her as inexperienced and unsuitable. "Stay away from me. Do not follow me again. Forget you even know me."

Ravensthorpe stepped around her, his footsteps crunching on the gravel path as he stormed away. She sagged against the prickly hedge behind her, more aroused than she'd ever dreamed possible.

Do you stroke your clitoris?

Was that the place between her legs that she rubbed in order to climax? She might not have learned the proper names, but she had explored her own body. She wasn't nearly as innocent as he thought.

And someday, now that she knew their attraction was reciprocated, she would prove it to him.

CHAPTER 2

I am destined for Hell.

Not that Max was a religious man, but the Devil himself was certain to come collect him for the dirty thoughts he harbored for Lady Violet Littleton.

He *burned* for her. So badly he could hardly stand to be in the same room with her. And she was wrong—he *always* noticed her. Since the moment she'd developed into a woman, Max hadn't been able to take his eyes off her. If they were anywhere in close proximity, his body remained in a permanent state of readiness, arousal simmering beneath the surface.

That was precisely how he'd known she was behind the hedge, watching him with Louisa. And then he, God forgive him, put on a prurient show meant to scare Violet away.

Yet he hadn't scared her.

Worse, she'd called him *Your Grace* in the high-pitched, breathy tone used by yielding lovers, those who adored nothing more than getting on their knees and taking whatever he was willing to give them.

Fuck.

He straightened his clothing and tried to compose himself. He was forty-one years old. Far too advanced to feel this twisted giddiness, this dark lust for a girl less than half his age. Hell, he had a son who was two years younger than Violet. Max was positively decrepit in comparison.

Not to mention that he'd fucked plenty of women since losing his virginity at the age of fifteen. Even more after his wife died while delivering their son. He had enjoyed a lifetime of debauchery and pleasure, hardly any of which he regretted. Moreover, he had no plans to give it up, not even for a fresh-faced virgin begging to ride his cock.

Jesus, her father would skin Max alive if he knew.

Max would need to adjust his social schedule for the remainder of the season to ensure Violet and he never attended the same event. It was for the best. She was far too tempting, especially now that she'd admitted her feelings for him.

Because I wished to take her place, Your Grace.

The statement had made him instantly, painfully hard, and it had been followed by a deep sense of shame. The girl was eighteen. A virgin. His friend's only daughter.

What the hell was wrong with him?

Max stepped inside the ballroom, not bothering to close the terrace doors. Charles Littleton, Lord Mayhew and Violet's father, grabbed Max's arm. "Ravensthorpe, have you seen my daughter?"

Charles was one of Max's close friends, a man he'd met shortly after arriving at school, long before he'd become Ravensthorpe. They had crossed cities and continents together, growing up in luxury, as many entitled aristocrats did. They knew each other's darkest secrets—well, all save one.

He forced his expression to remain blank. "No." Max held Charles's gaze like the competent liar he was, thanks to years in Parliament. "I was, ah, outside with Louisa." Not a lie.

Charles chuckled. "Of course you were, you bounder. Never one to pass up the opportunity for quality quim, are you?"

Uneasiness slid through Max. He reminded himself he'd done nothing untoward out there, at least not with Violet. "Cannot seem to help myself."

"I've an appointment myself tonight. Going to a little place on Holywell Street, one where they all wear masks. Perhaps you'd like to tag along?"

"I thought you said you were scaling back on your nocturnal activities after the missus discovered that you fathered a bastard."

"Well, what she doesn't know won't hurt anyone. So, what do you say?"

"Afraid I have plans, Mayhew. Have a pleasant time. If you'll excuse me."

Max had to get out of here. His skin was crawling with hunger for a girl he could not have. A woman, he supposed, but barely.

Violet was the type of gorgeous woman oblivious to her appeal, which in turn made her all the more appealing. An angel's face with a siren's body. Lush tits barely contained by any neckline, a round arse that beckoned with every stride. A woman built like a mistress, not a wife. In other words, utterly fuckable.

However, he was no green lad lacking in self-control. He could not pursue her. Even if the age difference did not bother him, there was the issue of his friendship with her father. While Max may have been a scoundrel, he was a loyal one. God knew he would not want his profligate friends anywhere near a daughter, if he had one.

No, Charles knew too much of Max's sordid history. Charles would reach for his pistol the instant after hearing word of his daughter in Max's bed. And Max wouldn't even bother to defend against such an egregious breach in friendship. He would deserve a bullet or two for defiling her.

Do you even know what it's like to make yourself come?

No idea why he'd asked such a crude question, other than to frighten her away, but it was clear by her reaction that she had touched herself. In the bath, perhaps? Or, had her seeking fingers drifted beneath the covers at night to stroke and circle her clitoris?

Blast. He had to stop or else he'd grow hard in the middle of this godforsaken ballroom.

Tonight, he would see Louisa and do all manner of wicked things to her. Moreover, he would forget about the blond beauty that haunted his dreams.

"Ravensthorpe."

Max stopped and found Louisa's husband, the Earl of Underhill, at his elbow. Hellfire and damnation. Was he conjuring these men through his illicit thoughts of the women in their lives? "Evening, Underhill."

Underhill wasn't a bad sort, actually. Louisa had been a penniless third cousin to a viscount before Underhill married her twelve years ago. More to the point, he was aware of Max's sexual relationship with his wife.

Underhill might even have been relieved over it, seeing as how the Underhills had stopped screwing eons ago.

And, as much as Max loathed it, his mistresses enjoyed an elevated social status during their time together. It had nothing to do with him and everything to do with his title. Still, husbands had been known to leverage that status a time or two, including Underhill.

Sodding aristocracy.

"Need a favor, Ravensthorpe."

Indeed, here came the leverage. "Oh?"

The skin above Underhill's cravat flushed, and he cleared his throat. "I suppose it is unusual considering the circumstances, but I, uh . . ."

Out of the corner of Max's eye he saw Violet slip into the ballroom. Awareness skated over every inch of him, his flesh hot and itchy under his clothes. He had to leave. Piercing the man across from him with a harsh glare, he barked, "Spit it out, Underhill."

The other man leaned in. "I need you to stop seeing Louisa. Just for a time. I'd like to start trying again for a son and, well, you understand."

He couldn't risk raising a duke's bastard. "Have you spoken to her about this?"

"No, but it is her duty to provide me with an heir."

Max smothered a sigh. He was disappointed, but probably not for the reason Underhill assumed. He needed the diversion of a woman closer in age, one who did not make him randy at every turn. Losing Louisa meant he needed to find another woman, fast. "Of course. There were plans for tonight, so . . .?"

"I'll take care of that. Appreciate it, Ravensthorpe."

"I wish you luck. She is a remarkable woman."

They parted and Max wanted to punch the wall in frustration. All he could do was pray his hand would suffice for tonight.

* * *

VIOLET'S FATHER found her almost the instant she slipped back into the ballroom. Papa was protective of her, especially in settings such as this. Perhaps it was because he was a rogue himself and knew the dangers that lurked during these night events. In fact, Mama frowned every time he left the house after dinner, as if she knew the illicitness he would seek out in those evening hours.

Violet and her parents had never been close. She'd never understood her father's philandering. Mama would yell and carry on, demand he stop seeing other women, and he would settle down for a few months. But the cycle soon repeated itself, her father incapable of remaining faithful, apparently. He never cared about the harm he caused, or the burden on his wife in enduring it.

For her part, Mama seemed unhappy, angry with everyone. Withdrawn. She refused to attend large social gatherings, even during Violet's debut, so Papa escorted Violet about instead.

"There you are," her father said. "You had me scared half to death. Where were you?"

Violet caught Ravensthorpe's tall form across the room where he was speaking with Louisa's husband. The duke appeared uncomfortable, his shoulders stiff and straight, looking nothing like the man who spoke seductive filth in secluded gardens.

You have every man panting after you the second you walk into a room.

"Violet," Papa snapped. "I asked you a question."

"I required fresh air. I went out on the terrace for a moment."

"It is unsafe for you to be there alone. Did you . . . see anyone?"

"No," she lied. "Not a soul."

Her father visibly relaxed. Had he known Ravensthorpe was outside?

"Good. Shall we leave, then?"

Ravensthorpe headed to the door, most likely leaving the ball. With the duke gone, there was no reason to stay. "Of course. I've had my fill of heated ballrooms."

"You are looking flushed. Are you all right?"

"I am?" She patted her cheeks. Was Papa able to see the lust on her face?

Lord Patton suddenly appeared at Papa's elbow. Patton bowed to Violet, his gaze lingering on her bosom in a manner that had her longing for a shawl. She'd never liked the man. He stood too close when speaking with her and found excuses to brush against her whenever possible. It made her skin crawl.

"The lovely Lady Violet." Patton reached for her hand, taking it before she could blink, and brought it to his lips. "Good evening to you, miss."

"My lord," she offered with a curtsy.

"Do you mind if I steal your father away for a moment?" Patton asked. "Then perhaps you'll honor me with a dance?"

She said the first thing that came to mind. "We were just on our way out."

Her father nodded. "We were leaving, but I'll only be a moment, Violet. Meet me by the front entrance, won't you?"

She excused herself and sighed in relief over evading Patton. Perhaps a stop in the ladies' retiring room was in order. At least there she could splash water on her face in an attempt to cool herself after the encounter with Ravensthorpe. The man possessed an uncanny ability to send her up in flames at the snap of his fingers.

The retiring room was empty. She took a moment to relieve herself and clean her hands. When she cracked the door, she discovered Louisa and her husband, Lord Underhill, behind a plant in the corridor, embroiled in what appeared to be a heated exchange. Had Lady Underhill's husband discovered her affair with Ravensthorpe?

Violet slowly retreated into the retiring room while keeping the door cracked ever so slightly for sound. Terrible of her to eavesdrop, but how could she help herself? This conversation could provide her with additional insight into Ravensthorpe.

"You will do what I say, Louisa," Underhill said, his voice low and sharp. "You will not see him again—not until I have an heir."

Violet sucked in a breath, then covered her mouth with a hand. So, Underhill knew of the affair and was forcing Louisa to call it off.

"Absolutely not," Louisa hissed. "You have no right to ask me to do so."

"As your husband, I do, actually."

"We've tried for a child twice without success. I have no desire to try again. It's exhausting."

"Understandable, as it's no picnic on my end, but that does not change the fact that we must do it. I've looked the other way on your affairs for years. This is the least you can do. Otherwise I'll be forced to move you out to the country. Try meeting your paramour way up there."

"You wouldn't dare."

"I'll have your bags packed tomorrow if you don't agree."

Violet's eyes widened. Between her parents and this couple, marriage seemed like a nightmare for wives. No fidelity or trust. Just threats and tantrums each way one turned.

"But I may return to him once I give you an heir?"

"Of course." Underhill actually sounded accommodating, as if he were doing her a favor. "Not that Ravensthorpe will wait for you."

"We have a bond you could not understand," she said—and Violet's stomach sank. Were there legitimate feelings between Ravensthorpe and Louisa? The possibility made Violet nauseous.

Underhill chuckled, but not with humor. "No doubt his wife thought the same before he caused her death. Besides, the man has screwed his way through the ton for years. You don't believe you are special to him, do you?"

"Again, you would not understand. I have kept his interest longer than most."

"Even still, do not find yourself surprised when he moves on."

"We have plans tonight. When I see him, I'll inform him that—"

"No need," Underhill interrupted. "I took care of it earlier when I spoke to him."

Violet leaned closer to the door, surprised. Lord Underhill had canceled the assignation with Ravensthorpe. Was that why the duke had appeared so uncomfortable on his way out?

Louisa gasped. "You had no right!"

"I beg to differ. I plan on getting started immediately, Louisa. And no doubt Ravensthorpe is wallowing in a Covent Garden bordello by now."

Was that where Ravensthorpe had gone? Out to visit a bawdy house? Violet's throat tightened, choking on the possibility that she might never be alone with him again.

"He despises those types of establishments," Louisa said. "Which is why I know he'll wait for me."

A group of women came laughing and chatting around the corner, likely headed for the retiring room. To avoid being caught eavesdropping, Violet pushed open the door and walked into the corridor. Lady Underhill brushed by as if headed for the ballroom, while her husband had already turned away, drifting deeper into the house. Violet's mind spun with possibility as she nodded at the blur of young ladies as they passed, not really noticing them.

Would Ravensthorpe return to sit in his house, alone? Or would he find feminine companionship elsewhere?

If he were at home . . . would the side door be unlocked, even with his cancelled plans?

No, she couldn't.

Could she?

He would never allow Violet inside . . . but what if she didn't ask? What if she surprised him? He was attracted to her—he'd admitted it outside—and she might convince him to act on it, if they were alone together. Isolated, where no one would find them.

The moment felt fortuitous. Momentous. Everything she wanted—a chance with Ravensthorpe—was dangling right in front of her like a sweet treat. She merely had to be bold enough to take it.

Was she content to wait around and hope he noticed her again?

Your body is made for sin and your face would make angels weep.

One thing was perfectly clear: he would never come to her. He had ordered her to stay away from him, had pushed her to find a man her age. She would need to take matters into her own hands.

Did she dare?

CHAPTER 3

*M*ax lounged in the darkness of his study, legs angled toward the fire as he sipped the most expensive brandy his vast amounts of money could buy. He'd long lost track of the time, the chime of the clock forgettable since he arrived home. His plans for the evening were ruined, and he hadn't been able to do much of anything except sit and brood.

I could be fucking her right now.

He shouldn't think it, shouldn't even let the hint of it cross his mind. He should imagine screwing Louisa instead, with her bold caresses and wicked tongue—not a girl barely out of the schoolroom.

And yet.

The brandy lowered his defenses, and Violet crept into his mind like a vine that burrowed under his skin to hold and drag him down. He couldn't resist wondering and speculating, his mind storing a mental list of all the depraved things he'd do to her glorious body if but given the chance.

This had to stop. Lusting after her like this caused him to feel like a filthy old man. Many dukes in their twilight years married young girls, but Max had secretly sneered at those pathetic louts. Yes, they all needed heirs—Max had already scaled that particular mountain—but there were plenty of seasoned women who could bear children. One need not marry a girl barely more than a child herself.

His eyes drifted to the mound of paperwork on his desk. His nights with Louisa were necessary diversions, an escape from the responsibilities of his life. To pleasure and be pleasured in return, to let his mind focus on something other than numbers.

You're lonely.

He snarled at the fire, as if the voice had come from the flames. The idea was ludicrous. He was invited everywhere, had his pick of bed partners, and there was Will, his sixteen-year-old son and heir. Will was away at school, off to Eton as all young aristocratic males did at his age.

Will had been the center of Max's world for so long. Since the boy's birth, Max had kept his son close and made certain to spend time with him, to show Will how much his father loved him. Then perhaps Will would not hate him when he came to learn the circumstances of what happened to his mother. How Max had utterly failed as a husband.

He didn't want another wife or any more children. Ever. He had an heir and, thanks to Max's proficiency on the Exchange, Will would inherit more money than God when Max died, not to mention a dukedom. Ducal duty had been fulfilled. Max never needed to go through that again.

He did, however, need another mistress. This required an immediate search, though there were some options. Such as the viscountess who had propositioned him at the opera last month, or the Spanish princess he'd flirted with at the palace dinner weeks ago. As well, his former mistress, Georgina, had written recently in the hopes of reestablishing their association.

None of them caused his blood to race, unfortunately.

That's because you want her.

Christ, this had to stop. He downed the rest of the brandy in his snifter and debated pouring a fourth. He had a meeting with his estate manager in the morning and a hangover would only make the bloody business take longer.

The scrape of metal caught his attention. Someone was slowly opening his study door.

No servant would dare to enter without knocking. This could only be one person, and Max's mood picked up considerably.

Louisa. She'd found a way to sneak off from her husband after all.

Fortunate that he'd unlocked the side door earlier, despite Underhill's warnings.

Relief flooded him. A distraction was exactly what he needed, and he should reward her a bit for coming. Louisa liked when he ignored her and she had to beg for his attentions. Max didn't mind. What man wouldn't want a beautiful woman begging him to fuck her?

Playing coy, he focused on the glass in his hands, twirling the empty crystal in the firelight. Slippers moved across the carpets, skirts rustling, and lust sparked in his belly as he contemplated what was to come. Louisa rarely wore drawers and kept the hair on her mound trimmed short. Was she already wet and eager for him?

The outline of a black cloak caught the corner of his eye. She'd come prepared like a thief in the night. Underhill wouldn't like this, but one last time as a way to say good-bye properly wouldn't hurt, would it? Max wasn't fully hard, but it wouldn't take much to excite him, not after his encounter with Violet.

Because I wished to take her place, Your Grace.

No, not now. He could not think of her *now*.

Louisa stopped just out of his reach, her face turned away from him, toward the fire. She trembled slightly, anticipating his touch, and he relished the reaction. It made him feel more powerful than any man on earth. "I see you escaped," he said, his voice a low rasp. "Are you here to play?"

The hood moved as she nodded.

"I like that you couldn't stay away from me. Needy little thing, aren't you?"

Another nod.

In deference to Underhill's request for an heir, Max said, "I cannot fuck you tonight, sadly, but I do plan to enjoy you in every other way possible."

She was quiet, but he could almost feel her vibrating with excitement. Normally, Louisa would break character about now with a giggle or urging him to hurry. She was showing incredible restraint . . . and he meant to honor that effort by giving her unimaginable pleasure.

"Bend over that chair," he said, pointing to the plush armchair opposite his. "Fold yourself over the arm."

For a second, she hesitated. Then she walked over and draped her front over the side of the chair, arse in the air, with her face hidden.

"Such a good girl," he praised, unfolding from his seat and rising. "Now, lift your skirts."

She struggled awkwardly with her skirts, almost as if she were shy. Or innocent.

Lust unwound in Max's groin, a slow warmth that traveled along the backs of his legs and through his bollocks. He didn't care to question as to why her performance aroused him—he was terrified of the answer—so he just accepted that it did.

"Higher," he barked when she paused. "Show me."

Damn, it was as if they'd switched and were now catering to his fantasies. His cock lengthened, pushing against his underclothes. Her calves and the backs of her knees were already bared to his gaze, and he saw the lace of her drawers peeking out to tantalize him.

His skin hummed with a familiar sensation, one he'd experienced at the ball, but he forced it away. This was no time to let those thoughts intrude. That particular young woman wasn't here and he needed to focus on the woman in front of him, to continue their games until they were both exhausted and dripping with sweat. "I see you are a tempting little minx tonight," he growled, dragging a finger along her spine.

She moaned softly and he couldn't wait a second more. Dropping to his knees behind her, he shoved her skirts out of his way. "Spread your legs," he ordered, and hurriedly stripped off his waistcoat. Gripping her inner thighs, he pushed her open further. He couldn't see much in the dim firelight, but the lips of her quim glistened with arousal, causing his mouth to water. Leaning in, he dragged his tongue through her folds.

The heavenly taste, a sweet and musky flavor, exploded on his tongue just as bells went off in his head, a clamoring that something was very wrong. The feel of her body was different. The smell of her skin was not the usual vanilla and lavender, but rather lemon. The hair on her mound was longer. The drawers . . .

Bloody hell.

Shoving himself away from her, he fell back on his arse, skittering on his limbs like a bloody crab, desperate to put distance between them.

No, no, no. She hadn't. *He* hadn't. This could not have happened.

"Turn around," he choked out, dread pressing on his chest. "Turn the fuck around, right now."

Legs shaking, she slowly straightened and let her skirts fall. Then she faced him . . . and Max's stomach dropped.

Violet.

"You." Blood rushed in his ears as he stared up at her, unable to believe it. "What in God's name have you done?"

Red bloomed on her cheekbones and she stared at his shoes. "Is it not obvious?"

"Not to me. Spit it out, Violet. Why have you come here tonight, sneaking into my house and making me believe you were someone else?"

"I never said I was her." Her head snapped up and she straightened, almost defiant. "And I thought you saw my face."

Fury raced through his veins like a lit fuse, sending flames to every part of his body. He nurtured it, grateful to replace the other unwelcome emotions from a moment ago. "A lie if I've ever heard one. As far as you knew, Louisa was coming tonight and you tried to take her place."

"I knew she wasn't coming. I overheard her husband telling her that she could no longer see you."

"So you draped yourself in a cloak, thinking I wouldn't know the difference between you and her. One cunt is just as good as another, is it?"

She flinched, but he would not apologize. Just having her taste on his tongue, picturing her bent over his armchair, had him balancing on a precarious edge. He wanted her too badly for politeness.

"You were able to tell the difference just from . . . that?"

God save him from innocent virgins. "We men are simple creatures, but yes. Even we are capable of recognizing the woman we are currently fucking from behind."

"*Were* fucking," she corrected with a knowing smirk. "Seeing as how her husband has now forbidden it."

The little she-devil was entirely too pleased with herself, and he liked this brazen side of her. A lot. Which meant he had to distance himself from this young woman at all costs. "Get out, Violet. Before we both do something we will regret."

"Did I . . ." She took a deep breath and let it out in a rush. "Did I not taste acceptable to you?"

The conscience he'd long forgotten chose that moment to rear its ugly head. He could have cut her down with a few simple words, destroyed her newfound confidence and probably sent her from the room in tears. But he couldn't do it. Nor would he lie, not about this. "You tasted like the sweetest ambrosia. I could spend a week doing nothing but licking you to orgasm and not tire of it."

Desire darkened her eyes and she swayed on her feet, a tiny gasp escaping her lips. Goddamn, she was magnificently responsive. So easily affected by him. More blood pumped to his groin, his cock hardening further beneath his clothing. He wanted nothing more than to dive beneath her skirts once again, hear her cries of delight ringing in his ears.

She is Charles's daughter.

Only eighteen.

He will never forgive you.

You cannot marry her.

With her taste in his mouth and the image of her naked quim in his brain, the usual reasons why he should stay away from her weren't working. He resorted to pleading with her. "Please, Violet. You should—"

"Did I cause that?" She pointed to the obvious erection between his legs.

"Yes," he answered without thinking. "But you should not know of such things, little mouse."

"May I see it?"

Every muscle froze and all the moisture fled his mouth. *Oh, Christ.* What was she trying to do to him? He'd end up in an asylum before the end of the night at this rate. Why was she not fleeing his house in terror?

Because she's far stronger than you've imagined, you dolt.

He swallowed. "If you cannot even say the word, then you are not ready to see it." His voice came out husky and teasing, not the biting tone he'd imagined in his head.

Violet must have sensed his weakness, because she took one step closer. "May I see your cock, Your Grace?"

His lips parted, his breath sawing out of his chest, short and swift. The question and the honorific uttered in her pliant, pleasing voice were his undoing. He'd tried so hard, but he wanted her too badly. Craving sizzled in his veins, like an addict denied his pipe, and Max could deny it no longer, whatever the consequences.

He let his lips curve into a sly smile full of wickedness. "You may, but you must take it out first."

CHAPTER 4

*V*iolet had never been so scared in her whole life. But there was something underneath the trepidation, an emotion that emboldened her and turned her into a wanton creature worthy of Ravensthorpe. Perhaps it was longing or passion, or the ravenous desire he inspired in her. Whatever it was, he seemed to appreciate it.

Even while angry with her, Ravensthorpe made her feel safe. Protected. Like she could say or do anything and he'd not judge her harshly for it. Which was probably why, despite her inexperience, she wasn't afraid of whatever was happening between them.

He remained sprawled on the study floor, his long limbs akimbo as he studied her, the erection in his trousers enticing her to come and play. Firelight danced off the sharp angles of his face, the glow reflecting off the silver strands at his temples. He was irresistible and shameless, and the darkness only enhanced his appeal.

Ravensthorpe said nothing, his chest rising and falling with the force of his breaths. Though he was on the ground, he was clearly still in control of the room, like a jungle cat taking a momentary break to tease its prey, daring her to approach him.

Did he believe she wouldn't follow through?

Flicking open the clasp on her cloak, she shrugged off the heavy cloth and let it fall. Then she lifted her skirts and dropped to her knees, the carpet soft beneath her stockings. Without a word, he widened his legs, making room for her between them, so she shuffled forward, her heart pounding behind her corset.

When she reached his thighs, he growled, "Unfasten my trousers."

With trembling fingers, she reached to do as asked. Her nail traced the edge of the wide black button before slipping it through the hole. There were more buttons underneath, so she carefully undid each one around his bulging erection. Her fingers brushed his belly, the brief contact making him jump. She pressed her lips together to keep from grinning. *I affect this gorgeous man with a simple touch.*

"Now the braces."

He made no move to assist her, only held perfectly still as she slipped one brace over his shoulder, then the other. When she finished, she sat back on her knees and waited for him to continue with instructions.

"My shirt."

His collar and necktie had already been removed, so she leaned in once more and set to work on the small buttons on his chest. His lean muscles rippled beneath her fingers, the carefully leashed power betrayed by his rapid breathing.

When enough buttons were loosened, she dragged the expanse of fabric over his head, Ravensthorpe lifting his arms to help. The thin garment he wore underneath was of the finest cloth, and it outlined the thick muscle and sinew, the flat planes and elegant grace. Another wave of heat rolled through her, centering between her legs.

More.

She was greedy when it came to this man. Dark need buzzed beneath her skin, a yearning to see every bit of him.

When she stared too long, he said, "The undergarment, Violet."

Instead of unbuttoning the garment at his chest, she reached for his groin. After all, they both knew what she was after, considering she'd asked to see it.

Behind the opening in his trousers, she found small buttons and began working them open. He didn't speak but she could feel him watching, his intense gaze like a caress over her breasts, along her center. Would he lick her again? Because that one swipe of his tongue between her legs had felt like heaven.

Bare skin appeared as she continued, her first peek at the man underneath the polished exterior. She could hardly breathe for all the excitement coursing through her.

"That's it," he said, his voice a silky whisper, and her body shivered under his encouragement.

More.

She purposely paused, just so he would start talking again.

"Keep going. Just one or two more, my little mouse."

Oh. She pressed her thighs together, nearly groaning under the weight of her longing. She would do anything if he kept speaking to her like that and calling her his. Her hands moved faster now, following his direction as if she'd been born to do it.

Reclining onto his elbows, he lifted his hips slightly as she tugged his trousers low on his hips. Fabric shifted on his stomach, and his erection emerged from between the open sides of his undergarment. His penis sprouted proud and thick from a patch of dark, coarse hair, and she stared at it, fascinated by its reddish cap and smooth, tight skin.

Their breathing and the pop of the fire were the only sounds in the room. Was he assuming she'd run screaming from the house? Hardly. The sight of him made her mouth water. If only she had her photography equipment. . .

She licked her lips, uncertain but definitely eager. "What do I do?"

His dark eyes glittered from underneath his long lashes. "You worship it."

Yes, yes, yes. Indeed, that she could do.

He watched carefully, every bit of his attention on her, and she vowed not to disappoint him. She dipped to press a kiss to the head of his shaft, not looking away from his eyes. His lips parted and she heard him give a swift intake of breath. Emboldened, she touched her tongue to the same spot, and he hissed a very creative curse.

He reached down, gripped the base with his elegant fingers, and angled his cock toward her mouth. "Suck."

She wrapped her lips around the plump head and drew him in. His entire body tensed. "More. Take me deep."

Pressing down, she slid him as far back as she could manage. He tasted clean and musky, so firm and silky on her tongue. It was much better than she'd ever imagined. She repeated the journey, noticing how his cock jerked when her tongue glided over the skin underneath the head. The next pass was slower, with more attention paid to that sensitive spot. His muscles clenched, and the reaction felt like a victory.

She worked hard then, moving faster to show him without words how much she wanted to please him. He grunted and rocked his hips, lost in the moment, until he suddenly lifted her up and away from his erection. In a blink, she found herself on her back, Ravensthorpe leaning over her, pressing her into the floor an instant before he sealed his mouth to hers in a punishing kiss.

This was no sweet melding of lips as described by poets and school-girls. No, he devoured her, his mouth immediately opening to give her his tongue. She took it eagerly, widening to allow him in, reveling in the slick heat as his tongue twined with hers. This kiss was a battle, a test. He was showing her all the passion, all the lust inside him, and she had to prove that she could accept it. Prove that she wanted it.

Violet never could resist a challenge.

She kissed him back just as eagerly, with just as much fervor, their lips and teeth crashing into one another as their mouths worked. It was messy, almost angry, and she loved every minute of it. Ravensthorpe kissed as if he could bend the world to his will through this alone, and she wasn't entirely sure he couldn't.

Tearing his mouth away, he slid his lips down the column of her throat. "I might not ever recover from the sight of my cock between your lips, sweet girl."

Her back arched as he bit her skin, his teeth digging deep to mark her, and wetness pooled between her legs. She dug her nails into his back.

Without warning, he sat up. For a moment she worried they were done, but he let his gaze travel the length of her. "I want you naked," he growled. "Here in my study."

"Yes," she breathed, ready to give him almost anything if he'd just continue kissing her.

Relief flashed over his expression, as if he'd feared she would deny him. He made a motion with his hand. "Roll over."

* * *

MAX HELPED Violet turn onto her stomach. He wouldn't take things far tonight, but whatever happened, he would damn well ensure that Violet enjoyed it. Nothing else mattered at the moment.

Quickly, he unfastened her bodice and unlaced her corset. Untied her bustle and skirts. He was no stranger to women's clothing, well familiar with the tapes and hooks, and the process took hardly any time at all. Violet remained on her stomach, lifting when he ordered, allowing him to disrobe her.

With the outer layers removed, she was down to a chemise, drawers, and stockings, all white with pink satin ribbons. Perfect skin glowed underneath, the shape of her tempting him, an outline of the curves he'd imagined for months. The tip of his cock leaked, his bollocks aching with the desire to pump inside her. To defile and pleasure her. To *ruin* her.

You cannot fuck her. You cannot marry her.

But he could do everything else.

"On your back."

She turned over, giving him the perfect view of her ample tits. Full and ripe, the creamy mounds spilled out over her chemise, the berry-tipped nipples jutting against the thin fabric. Her chest heaved with her excitement, thrusting her breasts higher, and Max's mouth went dry.

He clenched his fists and contemplated rending the flimsy fabric in half. "Take off your chemise."

She did as he asked, wriggling her hips and shoulders, revealing her bare torso to his greedy gaze. Fuck, she was perfect, with curves exactly where he liked them. His hands shook as he reached for her, his sanity slipping. "If I do something you don't like, tell me and I'll stop. All right?"

She nodded, but that wasn't enough. "The words, Violet. Tell me you understand."

"I understand, Your Grace."

She peeked at him through her lashes, shy but emphasizing his honorific, and he couldn't bring himself to care. He fell on her like a man possessed, kissing her hard and deep, needing her like he'd never needed anyone before in his life.

Before the weight of that thought could bring him down, he moved to take the tip of her breast into his mouth, drawing deep. His hand cupped the supple flesh as he licked and sucked, loving the little whimpers she gave before he moved to the other breast to give it the same attention.

Her nipples were thick, each surrounded by a large areola, and he adored the way they felt on his tongue. When she was writhing under him, moaning loudly, he pulled back to admire her. The suction from his mouth had caused her nipples to puff even more.

Jesus, everything about this girl was so damn arousing.

"You are absolutely gorgeous," he muttered as his hands went to her drawers. "But you still have on far too much clothing."

In a flash, he divested her of her drawers and stockings, marveling that she hadn't yet shied from his touch or tried to cover herself. She seemed to want him every bit as much as he wanted her. Surely that wouldn't last. It couldn't.

It never did. His former duchess had proven that, hadn't she?

So he would enjoy this with Violet while he could.

When she was naked, he sat on his haunches, marveling at the picture before him. Lush breasts, smooth skin, generous hips that would cushion his own perfectly . . . and her mons with its delicate triangle of hair. No man had explored there, and while Max knew he didn't deserve to be the first, he was bastard enough not to refuse it.

"Spread your legs. Show me."

Those pale thighs parted, revealing her pussy, and he couldn't breathe. *Goddamn beautiful.* Arousal glistened on the petals, with more gathered around the entrance. He traced the soft flesh with a fingertip, relishing the slick her body produced for him. "Is all this for me?" She watched him with wide eyes as he brought the finger to his mouth and sucked the sweetness onto his tongue. "Oh, my darling girl. I fear I'll never get enough of your taste."

Dropping onto his stomach, he let his breath tease her until she started to squirm. Then he began licking her, gently at first, getting her used to the feel of a tongue between her legs. The taste was exquisite, tart and musky, and he felt like a fifteenth-century explorer on a voyage of discovery and delight into unchartered lands while she gasped and mewled beneath him. His cock leaked onto the carpet, the skin pulled so tight it hurt, and yet he somehow resisted the urge to hump the floor.

When his attentions focused directly on her clitoris, her entire body twitched. "*Your Grace!*"

He swirled his tongue over that swollen bud, loving it with his teeth and mouth, sucking and laving until she trembled. One of her hands found its way onto the back of his head, where she held him in place, fingers clutching his hair, and nothing made him prouder than his little mouse demanding her pleasure.

She was close, her body stretched like a bowstring, her chest pumping in a desperate plea for air. Max needed to feel her inexperienced walls clamp down, if not on his shaft, then on his finger. He carefully slid the tip of his smallest finger inside her cunt, and her slick walls sucked him inside as if starved. God, how he wished . . .

No. He could not even contemplate it.

Then it happened. Her thighs shook around his head, her cries ringing in his ears as she found her peak. The release went on and on, her body completely his in that moment, and the satisfaction he experienced as she climaxed on his tongue was incomparable.

When she relaxed, he removed his finger and continued to lick her, softer, relishing the additional wetness that now pooled at her entrance. So responsive, so delicious . . . he longed to do this until sunrise. But his bollocks were tight, almost painful, with the need for his own release. He feared he would spend on the carpets if he waited another moment.

Rising onto his knees, he took his cock in hand and stroked, admiring her luscious form the entire time. Christ, she was beautiful. "Play with your breasts," he ordered, little electric shocks of lust shooting through his groin. "Pinch your nipples."

Her hands crept to her tits, cupping them as if offering them up to him. Then she squeezed the tips, her mouth rounding in surprise, as if she'd never touched them so intimately before. Her innocence—not to mention her willingness to do as he said without question—drove him positively wild. "More," he grunted, his hand moving faster along his shaft.

She watched his hand, seeming fascinated, as she rolled and tweaked her nipples, her tongue swiping across her lower lip. Was she thinking of sucking on him again? Swallowing his spend down her throat? God, the idea of it . . .

"Fuck," he gasped, sensation overtaking him, heat sizzling along nerve endings, and spend erupted from the top of his cock to land on her stomach. He clutched her thigh to steady himself, his tight fist milking all the pleasure from his body while his limbs jerked and twitched. "So good, so damn *good*," he gritted through clenched teeth. He couldn't remember the last time he came this intensely, as if his entire body were being wrung inside out in pleasure.

Each blissful pulse washed over him, renewing and reenergizing, breathing new life into his old and tired brain. He never wanted this feeling to end.

Yet it soon did. His faculties returned slowly, and with them came the dawning horror as to how low he'd sunk.

I've debauched her. Touched her when I hadn't the right.

Taken another innocent girl and horrified her with my base ways, just like Rebecca.

He hung his head, unable to look at her. What had he done?

CHAPTER 5

"*T*his was a mistake."

Ravensthorpe's words, combined with the remorse stamped on his features, had Violet's stomach churning. This had been the best night of her life. She could not allow him to destroy what had happened between them with recriminations.

Yes, she'd come here in the hopes of seducing him, but she hadn't meant to trick him. Not really, anyway. While she may have tried to keep quiet at first, she hadn't known the room would be so dark, that he wouldn't see her face until . . . well, until it was too late. He'd made it clear at the ball he desired her. She'd planned to come tonight and give them a small nudge, to talk to him in private and convince him to give them a chance.

Of course, she hadn't realized Ravensthorpe would begin orchestrating a seductive play the moment she walked through the door. Not that she was complaining. The man merely had to open his mouth and she was at the ready, waiting like a good little soldier to follow his instructions.

And he believed this was a mistake?

Coming up on her elbows, she said, "I don't regret any of it. I'd do it again, in fact."

The duke dragged a hand down his face. "Violet, you cannot possibly—"

"Stop. Do not dare tell me I cannot understand. I have much more to lose than you by being here, and I am well aware of the possible repercussions."

"I won't marry you."

She flinched. The reminder was meant to put distance between them, and it worked. Pushing aside the sudden ache surrounding her heart, she reached for her stockings and pulled them on. "I haven't asked for marriage, Your Grace."

He mumbled something under his breath.

"I beg your pardon?"

"I said to call me Max."

He was giving her leave to use his given name? That had to mean something, didn't it? "I haven't asked for marriage, Max."

Head down, he began putting his clothing back to rights. She ignored his unhappy expression and studied him instead, from his wide shoulders and strong arms, to the perfectly sculpted flat chest. Even partially dressed, he made her heart flutter.

If she ever saw him completely naked, she'd likely faint from lust.

She was tying her drawers when he moved to still her hand. His gaze was soft, but filled with resolution. "Let me help you."

Her body melted at his sudden tenderness, and she leaned back to let him proceed. When he'd finished tying the ribbons, he ran the silk through his fingertips. "Pink and delicate. I think you wore these to drive me mad."

Before she could ask what he meant, he righted her chemise and dropped it over her head. He smoothed the fabric down, taking extra care at her breasts. "A shame to cover these beauties." One finger traced her right nipple slowly, almost reverently, and the flesh quickly puckered under the attention.

"My God," he murmured. "I do love the way your body responds to me."

Because you are the only man I've ever wanted.

She didn't dare say it, however. Not while he considered tonight a mistake.

She knew otherwise. This evening had proven how much he desired her, how explosive they were together. Nothing about coming here had been a mistake.

They hardly spoke as he assisted her with the corset and bustle, the petticoats and dress. The emotional distance grew as more and more layers of clothing separated their bodies. After he handed her the black cloak, he gestured to the door. "I'll see you out."

The sentence held a note of finality, that this was the last time, and the possibility terrified her.

She dug in her heels. "When will I see you again?"

He sighed and shoved his hands in his trouser pockets. "You won't."

Pain ripped through her chest and settled behind her ribs. "Max—"

"Do not argue with me, Violet. We've satisfied our curiosity and that was that. This is not an affair."

"I am far from having my curiosity satisfied—and it could be an affair, if you'd but allow it."

"You ask the impossible," he said, his voice low and angry. "And one day you'll thank me for preventing it."

"Because you believe you're too old for me."

"I *know* I am too old for you. And your father would never—"

"My father hardly has a moral ground upon which to stand. You of all people probably know that better than most."

Max shifted and did not bother to deny it. She'd hit her mark, then. Indeed, Max was privy to her father's sins. "Nonetheless, he is your father and my friend. An affair between his daughter and me is impossible."

She hated how rational and calm he sounded, as if his mind were made up. What happened to the wild lover of moments ago, the one spewing filth from his mouth and clutching her as if he never wanted to let go? "Are you saying you've never slept with a woman more than twenty years your junior?"

His expression darkened at the reminder of their age difference. Stalking away, he grabbed the decanter on the side table and refilled an empty glass. After taking a large swallow of what had to be brandy, he said, "I haven't, actually. I make a habit of choosing experienced women who needn't be shown how to pleasure a man."

The wounded lion lashes out.

Violet was not fooled. This man had nearly fallen at her feet moments ago, dazed by her kisses and drunk on her taste. His body's reaction to her couldn't have been faked, so she knew her innocence hadn't bothered him. In fact, she would guess the opposite based on his rabid ardor—that he'd enjoyed instructing her.

Confidence surged through her like a great gust of air and filled her with newfound knowledge and purpose. She lifted her chin. "Perhaps I'll find a young buck to teach me, then. I'll return after some tutelage and you might reconsider."

His gaze, possessive and dark, narrowed on her. "Do not even contemplate it, Violet."

"Or?"

"Or I'll put a stop to it. And beat whomever you've convinced to help you within an inch of his miserable bloody life."

She bit her lip to hide her smile. Oh, yes. This was far from over between them.

"Stop looking so pleased with yourself," he snarled. "I will only destroy you and never marry you. Consequently, you should run from this house and never look back."

"And yet I cannot."

"I do not want you to return. Is that clear enough for you?"

The words were like spikes through her heart, tearing the tender flesh straight through, but she would remain strong. He was stubborn . . . yet so was she. "I think you're lying."

His lips flattened into a thin, angry line. "I've pummeled men for lesser insults than the one you just handed me."

"You won't hurt me. I've known you nearly all of my life."

"You know nothing about me."

Yes, I do. I see you. I've always seen you.

She had observed him carefully during her parents' dinner parties. Well read and intelligent, Max could speak to almost any topic, no matter how obscure. He was also kind and thoughtful. He made certain to escort elderly Aunt Harriet, who had difficulty walking unassisted, and he doted on his son, refusing to ship the heir off to boarding school when William was a young boy.

Now she'd discovered more about the allegedly wicked Duke of Ravensthorpe. His sweetness. His giving heart. His jealousy when she mentioned other men.

He believed he would destroy her, but that was impossible. Tonight she had discovered herself . . . and Max had helped her do it.

"We shall see," she said, cryptically.

"Goddamn it. You must listen to what I am saying."

Yes, she was listening, and one thing was perfectly clear—she could no longer chase him. She had to give Max space and let him come to her instead. Whatever was between them only worked if they were both amenable, both willing to take risks for the other. As it was, she had risked enough for him.

What if he moves on without you?

It was a gamble, certainly. No telling how many women were angling to get in his bed. And yet, everything inside her screamed this was the right choice.

"I'll see myself out," she said and turned to the door.

"You are not leaving until you agree never to return."

She paused and tried to remember this was for the best. Either way, win or lose, she couldn't pursue Max like a hound after a fox forever. "I won't return until you invite me."

Glancing over her shoulder, she gave him a heated look from under her lashes. "Because you will come looking for me, *Your Grace*. And when you do, I'll be waiting."

* * *

Fourteen days.

It had been fourteen days since the night in his study, the moment when Violet had turned his world upside down, and now Max worried he was losing his mind.

He couldn't stop thinking about her, couldn't stop remembering their night together, and somehow the girl had burrowed under his skin with her shy smiles and bawdy demands. So eager, so brave. Looking up at him as if he were a good man, one capable of solving any problem on earth.

And he most definitely had gone mad, because he was currently circulating the social event of the evening whilst searching for a blond-haired she-devil.

This is a mistake.

Yes, entirely. He could readily admit it, yet he could not stop himself.

For a week he'd held out, staying busy with his accounts and clubs. By day nine he'd begun drinking heavily, fisting his cock as he relived the memories of her kiss and the feel of her skin.

Day eleven had found him at one of the city's high-end brothels, one he hadn't visited in ages. He'd turned around and left before even removing his coat. How could he fuck another woman with the taste of Violet still fresh in his brain?

By the end of day twelve, he was stalking his London home like a starved dog, snarling at anyone who dared bother him. He locked himself in, convinced that Violet was a fever in his blood, one he merely needed to ride out. Then she would be out of his system forever and he could get on with his life.

It hadn't worked.

Now he was broken, unable to concentrate. An utter mess of a human being. A man on the verge of hysteria.

Just once more, he'd promised himself earlier today. If he could touch and kiss her just once more, that would be enough to get her out of his head. Then he could set her free, where she could marry anyone she pleased.

He was doing her a favor, really. Most young women—his deceased wife included—came to the marriage bed completely ignorant and unprepared. Max would leave Violet a virgin but at least teach her about sex and her own pleasure.

God, you're pathetic. You're attempting to justify bedding an eighteen-year-old woman.

Yes, but he was too far gone. He'd beg if necessary. Everything about her had been too perfect, too right. It had been the most erotic night of his life, one he couldn't help but relive every time he closed his eyes.

She was confident for her age, self-assured in ways that had surprised him. When was the last time he'd been surprised? Perhaps his liaisons had becoming boring of late, more rote than exciting, but Violet had energized his existence. She made him feel ten years younger and more randy than a university lad in a bordello.

"Ravensthorpe."

Max froze at the sound of the familiar voice, making sure to wipe his expression clean. He'd avoided Violet's father since the night in his study, uncertain how he could face his friend after what had occurred. The only good part about seeing Mayhew meant that Violet was likely in the room, as well.

He cleared his throat and spun around. "Mayhew."

Charles slapped Max's shoulder. "Haven't seen you in ages. Where have you been keeping yourself?"

At home, dreaming of fucking your daughter.

Instead, he said, "Here and there."

"Heard Louisa gave you the shove-off, my friend. A shame, indeed. Have you already found someone new?"

Max suppressed a wince and adopted an easy smile. "Not as of yet, no."

Charles leaned in closer and lowered his voice. "In that case, I'll happily show you a new place I've discovered. It's in Cheapside and the women are willing to do anything for the right price. And I do mean *anything.*"

After spending so many nights in Charles's company, Max had a good idea of what "anything" might include. "I believe I'm set for the moment, but I'll let you know. Are you here with your wife and daughter?"

"Just Violet. The missus is peeved with me again. Said I came home smelling like perfume too many nights this week."

My father hardly has a moral ground upon which to stand. You of all people probably know that better than most.

How much did Violet know about what went on between her parents?

Max frowned at his friend. "I hope you shelter your daughter from hearing such things. It could leave a damaging impression with her."

"Come now, she's a grown woman. I've got two suitors sniffing around her skirts, so best she learn how marriage works between a husband and a wife." Charles's brows lowered, his expression etched with disbelief. "Besides, you cannot tell me Will isn't aware of your mistresses."

Suitors? A dark cloud rolled through Max, his mood blackening at the thought of some repulsive masher pawing at that lovely girl. Scowling, he said, "Will is a man, not an impressionable young woman. And just who are these two suitors?"

"The young lords Wingfield and Sundridge. I had hoped Surrey would take an interest, but he seems enamored with the Gabriel chit's dowry."

"Wingfield undoubtedly has the pox and a bowl of porridge contains more intelligence than Sundridge. You cannot in good conscience encourage either of those fools."

"How on earth did you come by that information?"

His son, actually, who loved to gossip more than a maiden aunt, but Max didn't say as much. "Just know that I am right. She can do better, Charles."

Mayhew hooked his thumbs in his vest pockets. "Might not have much of a choice. The girl isn't exactly putting forth an effort. She stands against the wall and watches at every event. I never should have encouraged that photography habit of hers."

Photography? Violet was one of those Kodak Girls? He could almost picture her behind a camera, studying and observing. Laboring over her prints in a developing room. He hadn't much experience with photography himself, but he'd love to see her in action someday. "Perhaps you should put it off, let her experience this first season without pressuring her to marry. Then choose her a husband next year."

You are going to Hell, Max. Straight to Hell.

"Can't. I promised the missus we'd marry Violet off this year." Charles lifted a shoulder. "No idea why my lady is in such a rush, but I won't disappoint her—not on this."

Because he planned to disappoint his wife in other ways.

Max shifted on his feet and stifled the urge to say more. He had no right to interfere with Violet's future. After his own disastrous attempt at playing husband, he couldn't marry her—or anyone else—so he should just leave off, turn on his heel, and quit this bloody ball.

Yet he wouldn't. Because she was here, somewhere in this very room. And if he didn't find her soon, he might tear this ballroom apart with his bare hands.

Charles tipped his chin toward the dance floor. "Ah, I see Wingfield's claimed her for another dance. That's the second one tonight."

Max's head whipped toward the dancers, and he spotted her right away, her golden hair gleaming in the gaslight overhead. The breath locked in his lungs and he had to remind himself to breathe as he examined her. She was absolutely lovely in a cream silk evening gown with intricate beaded work covering the bodice. The delicate column of her throat was bare, begging for Max's mouth and hands.

That same sizzle whispered over his skin, like desire had commandeered his flesh, making him burn everywhere. *Once more. That's all I need.*

Wingfield's gaze drifted down to Violet's bosom, where it lingered far longer than was polite, and Max's hands curled into fists. Wingfield would need to be put in his place, it seemed.

"I'm headed to the card room," Charles was saying. "Care to join?"

"I'll pass. Excuse me," Max said, already drifting into the crowd. He moved to the edge of the dance floor, not bothering to hide as he caught Violet's eye. She stumbled when she spotted him—requiring Wingfield to steady her with a hand on her hip—and blinked.

Momentarily setting aside the need to pummel her dance partner, Max tilted his head toward the terrace. She nodded ever so slightly then looked away.

Excellent.

He ignored those who attempted to catch his attention as he strode through the crush. The whole world could wait, as far as he was concerned.

Now was time for play.

CHAPTER 6

*H*e was here.

Ravensthorpe was here and wished to see her. Violet could hardly believe it. Had her plan worked? It had been two weeks since their night together and she'd grown despondent, certain she'd erred in giving him space. So, she'd buried herself in her classes at the Polytechnic Institute and in her photographs. In fact, after so many hours in the developing room, the chemicals had begun to sting her lungs.

All that had been worth it, however, because the handsomest duke in London had arrived . . . and he'd motioned for her to meet him outside.

Her chest worked to draw in air, her corset growing tighter at the idea. Would he kiss her again? Goodness, she hoped so. She hadn't been able to stop thinking about their night together, the way he'd touched her, as if he already knew every part of her. As if they'd been together for years.

He thought he'd ruin her. Destroy her and toss her aside. Violet didn't believe it. She was safe with him, protected. Cared for. He'd pushed her away out of loyalty and an overblown sense of nobility, but perhaps he'd come to realize that he was safe with her, too.

Finally the music ended and Wingfield led her off the dance floor. "Lady Violet," he said, and she noticed the beads of sweat on his upper lip. "Would you do me the honor of joining me—"

"No, thank you, my lord. I must find my father. You'll excuse me?"

Without waiting on a response, she curtsied and then darted into the throngs of lords and ladies as she made her way to the French doors.

To Ravensthorpe.

Giddiness ignited in her chest like flash powder—and then Charlotte appeared in her path, a questioning expression on her friend's face. Violet stopped before she careened into the other woman. "Hello, Charlotte."

"You never finished telling me about your new suitor during our shopping trip yesterday." Violet's expression must've reflected her sudden panic because Charlotte continued. "Calm down. I meant Wingfield."

"Right." Violet exhaled in relief. "Wingfield."

Charlotte's brows lowered. "Who did you think I meant?"

"No one. Just unaccustomed to having a suitor, I suppose."

Her friend drew closer. "I am so happy to see you dancing. Three times tonight! For once you're not standing against the wall, watching everyone else."

Violet had no desire to converse at the moment. She tried to gracefully edge around her friend. "I don't know what's come over me. Perhaps I should get some air."

"Oh, excellent idea. I'm due for a dance, so I'll find you after." Charlotte squeezed Violet's hand and then disappeared into the crowd.

Violet wasted no time in hurrying to the French doors. She slipped onto the terrace, where cool night air washed over her exposed skin like a caress, causing her to shiver. With no torches or lamps outside, darkness engulfed her.

Strong fingers wrapped around her arm and began pulling her deeper into the gloom, helping her down the stone steps. She didn't need to see his face to know it was Max. His presence surrounded her, a feeling of safety and danger, arousal and comfort all at the same time. She went willingly, eagerly, unconcerned with getting caught.

Once on the ground, he tugged her into an alcove hidden underneath the stairs. Before she could see his face, he was on her, the muscular length of him flush to her front, her back against the rough stone.

But he didn't kiss her.

He put his mouth near her ear, his warm breath coasting over her skin. "Happy, little mouse? For two weeks I've tried to forget you. A goddamn fortnight, yet here I am—all because I cannot get the taste of your pussy out of my head."

Her lips parted on an exhale, his words both thrilling and arousing. Wetness gathered between her thighs, her pulse hammering in every bit of her sex. "Very happy, Your Grace," she whispered and slid her hands along the rigid slope of his chest.

"Christ," he bit out, bending to rock his hips into her thigh, his erection large and hard against her. She melted, her limbs growing languid. "I want to fuck you right here," he growled. "Turn you around and toss your dress above your head, bare you and sink inside."

"Yes," she gasped, definitely ready for that. There was emptiness, a place in her soul earmarked just for him, and she needed him to fill it.

"Hold your skirts."

"What?"

But he didn't explain, merely sank to his knees and began pushing layers of silk out of his way. He looked . . . possessed. Wild, like a starving man at a buffet. She moved to help, gathering the skirts in her arms until cool air washed over her stocking-covered legs.

Finding the part in her drawers, he lunged, pressing his face toward her sex, disappearing underneath layers of cloth. Then she felt the bold swipe of his tongue along her seam, and her knees wobbled as sensation jolted through her. His hands cradled her buttocks and lifted her left leg to place it over his shoulder.

"You must remain quiet," he ordered and dove under her skirts.

He wasted no time, licking and sucking until she whimpered. She thrashed her head as he tended to every part of her, driving her higher and higher, and lust tightened her muscles. He feasted, softly grunting in response to her moans, his mouth and tongue unrelenting, unforgiving against her flesh.

Voices suddenly sounded above on the terrace, a few revelers out for a bit of fresh air, no doubt.

Though she was well hidden, she froze, her chest heaving, and stared down at Ravensthorpe. The light of the moon revealed Max's smirk as he appeared from under her skirts. "Quiet," he mouthed, then returned to his task.

Sweet heavens.

She trembled under the onslaught, but her mind was stuck on the fact that they weren't alone out here. What if they were discovered? She tried to dislodge his face from between her legs, but the duke wouldn't budge. In fact, he doubled his efforts with her clitoris, sucking on the bud, laving it with his tongue.

It was too much.

Her eyes closed, the pressure building as fear and arousal mixed to overwhelm her, and she shoved her forearm into her mouth to stifle her cries as she came apart. Her body spasmed as her walls convulsed, white light exploding behind her eyes. When she regained herself, he gently dipped and swirled his tongue at her entrance, like he was trying to soak up every last bit of her taste.

Finally, he shot to his feet, his dark eyes glazed and hot. Her wetness coated his face and chin, and he licked his lips as he brought her hands to his waistband. "Finish me, Violet. Right now."

Oh, yes. She wanted that desperately. "What about . . ." She pointed to the terrace.

"They left. Hurry."

Swiftly, she unfastened his trousers and moved his shirtfront out of the way. "So many clothes." He made no move to help, staying perfectly still except for the breath sawing out of his chest.

She unbuttoned his undergarment and reached in, taking his shaft in her hand. The soft skin was stretched tight, her fingers unable to meet around his girth.

He dropped his forehead against her temple. "Squeeze hard," he said, giving a little thrust of his hips. "Stroke me. Fast."

Obeying, she tightened her grip and pumped his erection. He sucked in air and placed his hands on the wall behind her head. "That's it, my little mouse. Precisely like that."

He was so beautiful with his chiseled jaw and the few silver threads at his temple, his skin taut with excitement. She reached her other hand down to his testicles, rolled them in her palm, and Max let out a drawn out, "Fuck."

Hot breath hit her cheek as he began to talk. "We haven't long. Your father is in the card room and he'll come looking for you when he's done. I have the taste of you in my mouth. Would you like the taste of me in your mouth, as well?"

Her nipples tightened inside her clothing, and she rubbed her thighs together in a desperate bid for friction. Goodness, yes. She most definitely wanted that.

She started to lower to her knees, but he held her upright. "Wait."

He tore off his evening coat, folded it over, and dropped the cloth to the ground. She lifted her skirts and kneeled on his coat as Max began working his cock, rougher than she had, focusing almost entirely on the head. "Now, Violet," he gritted out, so she pressed forward and opened her mouth. Steadying her with a hand on her crown, he slid the head past her lips and groaned when she sucked. It took one swirl of her tongue and he reached his peak, his fingertips trembling on her scalp as spend coated the inside of her mouth.

"Yes," he gasped and shuddered. "That's it. Take it all."

She did, gladly. Her body sang in self-congratulatory pleasure as he climaxed, and when he finally pulled out she swallowed him down. Resting a palm against the hard stone, he lifted her chin with his free hand. His thumb traced her lips. "I expected you to spit but you didn't, did you?" He helped her stand then pressed his forehead to hers. "My God, Violet. What have I ever done to deserve you?"

He touched his lips to hers, kissing her softly, sweetly, with so much tenderness that she wanted to bottle it and hold onto the emotion forever. "Max," she whispered into his kisses, clutching him tightly. *"Your Grace."*

When they broke apart, he breathed, "Thank you, sweet girl," before stepping back. He tucked and smoothed her hair instead of righting his clothing. "There. Now you may return inside."

"What about you?"

"I'll go around the side and find my carriage. I've no desire to stand around a stuffy ballroom this evening."

Did that mean . . .? Giddiness flooded her chest, her heart swelling to a ridiculous size. "Did you come just to see me?"

"Go back to the ball." He began redressing, his attention on his buttons.

She shifted on her slippers, the gravel crunching beneath her feet. "When will I—"

"Inside, Violet." His tone was sharp and authoritative, the one he no doubt used when the Duke of Ravensthorpe wished to get his way.

But he was not the duke with her, not any longer. He was Max. He would not push her aside, especially when she still had the taste of him in her mouth. "Not until you tell me when I will see you again."

"We cannot do this." He pushed his shirtfront into his trousers. "It's too risky."

"Then let me come to your home."

"Violet—"

"Max," she snapped. "If you do not tell me precisely when, then I'll show up and surprise you."

"I won't let you in. I'll have the doors and windows locked at all times."

Silly man. She slid her hand up his chest, tucking her body close to his. "No, I don't think you will. In fact, I don't believe you'll last even fourteen days this time."

"Do not try to play games with me. You will lose."

She nipped his jaw with her teeth—and he shivered in response. Moving away, she whispered, "We shall see, Your Grace. We shall see."

* * *

Most days, Max avoided visiting his clubs. They were a waste of time, the rooms filled with brash young men barely older than Will, laughing and joking as if they hadn't a care. They caused Max to feel a hundred years old. Had he ever been so carefree, so jovial?

Not since assuming the title at fourteen, certainly. After a decade of wrangling the ducal accounts into shape, including taking risks on the London Exchange to refill the empty bank accounts, he'd been ready to do his duty. His choice of bride, the daughter of a high-ranking earl, had seemed a good one at the time, but he and Rebecca had been a poor match.

From the start, there had been problems in the bedroom. She preferred he not undress, and refused to let him see her without clothing. She remained perfectly still during the act, not complaining, but not participating, either. Kisses were to remain chaste and he was to leave immediately upon finishing.

Unhappiness had gnawed at him until Rebecca started increasing. Then he'd taken a mistress, relieved to finally enjoy himself with an eager partner. It had been selfish of him, a decision he'd regretted when his wife found out. Hysterical over his infidelity, Rebecca had gone into early labor and died whilst delivering Will.

A year into his marriage, Max was left widowed with a young son. And guilt. Plenty of guilt.

And the guilt hadn't yet subsided, not even sixteen years later.

None of it had been Rebecca's fault. Max should have been more patient, more understanding. He should have tried harder to explain his needs and desires, instead of rushing off to another woman's bed. Young and stupid, he leaped into marriage with the belief that a wife was no different than the other highborn ladies he'd slept with, the lusty widows and bored society wives.

But Rebecca had been different. It was Max who hadn't bothered to adjust his behavior, and he'd caused her death. Not a day went by when he didn't chastise himself over what he'd done, and he would repeat his pledge never to marry again.

Some men were not cut out to be husbands.

Still, he had no choice but to protect Violet.

Brooks's was quiet at this time of morning. After handing his hat and cane to the attendant, Max found his quarry in the main room, nursing coffee. Only a handful of men were spread out amongst the furniture.

Wingfield frowned at Max's approach. "Why must I be here so early, Ravensthorpe?"

Max slid into the chair opposite. "Because I wish to speak with you. And you are at my service, not the other way around."

Wingfield scowled but said nothing as he took another sip of coffee.

After an attendant brought Max a cup, they were alone again. Max came right to the point. "You will cease your pursuit of Lady Violet."

The young man's mouth fell open. "You have no right to—"

"I have every right," Max said icily. "I am a close family friend and have known the girl since she was born. You are not good enough for her."

"Not good enough for her?" Wingfield's voice rose several octaves. "The girl is the unequivocal flop of the season. I am doing her a favor by paying her attention."

His little mouse, a flop? Outrage roared through Max's veins like cannon fire, yet he tamped it down, hiding his emotions behind a bored expression. "You are a drunk and a spendthrift. Also, I have it on good authority that you've had mercury treatments—multiple times, in fact. You are not marrying Lady Violet."

Twin spots of scarlet dotted Wingfield's cheeks. "How dare you? My father—"

Max sighed loudly. "Your father is in debt to the West London Bank for hundreds of thousands of pounds. Would you care to guess the identity of that bank's largest shareholder?"

Wingfield sputtered. "Are you . . . Is this a threat?"

Christ Almighty, how was the world to survive with men this stupid?

"Yes," Max admitted, and then downed the rest of his coffee. "I am threatening you in order to keep you away from Lady Violet. Is that clear enough for you, Wingfield? Shall I put it in writing so there are no misunderstandings?"

Wingfield swallowed hard. "No, I understand. I'll stay away from her."

"Good." He rose. "See that you do."

Wingfield mumbled, "She's a stupid cow, anyway."

Max's entire body clenched and he leaned close to the younger man's face. "What did you say?"

"Nothing."

Max's hand shot out and he jerked Wingfield up by his collar, lifting the younger man until his feet barely touched the floor. Conversation in the room died, every eye turned their way. No one would dare say a word to stop Max, one of the most powerful men in Britain, from doing whatever he liked with this piece of filth.

"How dare you insult her." He tightened his fist, cutting off Wingfield's air supply. "If I hear of you talking about her, I will feed you to the pigs on my estate. Are we clear? You don't breathe her name ever again. If you see her on the street, don't even offer a polite greeting. She no longer exists for you."

Wingfield gasped, his eyes bulging, but Max didn't let up until the other man nodded. He let Wingfield go and straightened his cuffs. "Glad we understand each other."

With that, Max collected his things and strolled onto St. James Street. Instead of taking a hansom home, he decided to walk and clear his head. Rage from the encounter with Wingfield continued to burn through him, and he still had no idea what to do about Violet.

Two days had passed since the night of the ball . . . and he was already weakening. The craving for her lurked his blood, always present and growing stronger every minute.

I don't believe you'll even last fourteen days this time.

How had she known?

She was so certain about him, about *them.* The folly of youth, he supposed, not to understand the whole picture. He was bad for her, too old and too . . . rough. She deserved better. Someone sweet and kind, closer in age. Hell, Max would be lucky to live another twenty years. She needed a man who could marry her, give her children, and make her laugh into her old age.

Max was not that man.

Yet he wasn't certain he could stay away from her. He thought of her nearly all the time, his cock currently chafed thanks to his hand and his memories. Like a teenaged boy, he'd stolen a small jar of oil from the larder to protect his skin while pleasuring himself.

It would be funny if it weren't so mortifying.

As he crossed Piccadilly, he spotted a camera shop in the middle of the block. He recalled Charles mentioning Violet's interest in photography. Did she frequent this establishment?

She'd always been a clever and curious child, asking him questions about Will, the ducal estates, and anything else that crossed her mind during the Mayhew dinner parties. Math and history had been her favorite subjects, as he recalled, but they'd even debated philosophy at one point. Those qualities, along with her current voyeuristic tendencies, likely made her a stellar photographer.

Charles hadn't seemed appreciative of Violet's photography habit, but it was important to nurture hobbies, even for women. Perhaps especially for women, as they were told so often what they could not do, rather than be allowed to express themselves. Max would hate to see any of Violet's creativity stifled.

He was walking toward the shop before he could think better of it.

A bell chimed over the door as he entered. A middle-aged man emerged from the back and his eyes widened at the sight of Max. "Good morning. How may I help your lordship?"

Max didn't bother to correct the form of address. "I am interested in purchasing some photography equipment for a friend. Is there anything new or something you'd recommend?"

"I'd be honored. Has your lordship an idea of this gentleman's level of experience with photography?"

"It is a she, and no."

"I see. Then allow me to recommend this latest Kodak box model, the number one. Most women find it lighter and much easier to operate. It also comes pre-loaded with a flexible roll of film." The clerk pointed to a camera in the glass case. "It is our best seller."

"I'll take that, then."

"Excellent." The clerk withdrew a box from a locked drawer under the case. "Shall I wrap it for your lordship?"

Max considered this while he studied the other items in the case.

Have them deliver the camera with a note saying you cannot see her again.

The black heart in his chest instantly rejected the idea. He needed to watch Violet's face as she unwrapped his gift, see the youthful exuberance that hadn't yet been snuffed out by this harsh life. Drink in her happiness as if it were his own.

He wasn't ready to give her up.

You'll regret this.

Pushing aside his conscience, he handed the clerk his card. "If you would, yes. Have it delivered here."

The man's brows shot up. "Your Grace. Forgive me, I hadn't known. I shall see to it personally."

"Thank you." Max placed his bowler atop his head and left the shop, feeling lighter than he had in two days.

Soon, my little mouse. Soon.

CHAPTER 7

*V*iolet was in her dark room, developing photographs. She loved swirling the paper in the chemicals, watching the still image slowly take shape before her eyes, preserved forever. Memories that no one could take away, indisputable proof that someone had put their mark on this earth.

It required patience, which Violet had in abundance. After all, hadn't she waited years for Max to finally notice her? And now that he had, she'd never been happier.

What if I cannot change Max's mind about a relationship?

Then life would march forward. Women were more independent nowadays, at least outside of the ton. Perhaps she could convince her parents to let her live over her favorite camera shop in Chelsea in a set of small apartments. She could sell her photographs for money and support herself. Unless she could marry Max, there was no pressing need to find a husband.

I won't marry you.

If she couldn't change his mind, then she would suggest a long-time affair. Better to have Max in her life and suffer the social consequences than to live without him.

She removed the last photograph from the fixer bath and rinsed it in fresh water. Then she hung the paper on a line to dry along with the rest, taking a moment to appreciate it. This image might be her best yet. The light had hit the buildings perfectly, the women in the foreground sharp and clear. A perfectly captured London morning.

It took several minutes to clean up and remove her apron. Coming down the narrow attic stairs, she heard her parents arguing inside their bedchamber. She started to creep by, ensuring not to make a sound on the way to her room, when she heard her name.

". . . Violet's two suitors?" her mother shouted. "You are supposed to be hurrying them along."

Violet paused. Why were they discussing her marriage prospects?

"Only one now," her father said. "Wingfield's gone to Devonshire for the rest of the season."

Wingfield had left town?

"So marry her off to the other one. I need her settled, Charles. You promised me."

The other one? Violet had no idea who they were discussing.

"I don't know, Elsie. Sundridge seems a bit dim."

Violet put a hand over her mouth. Sundridge? He'd called her Victoria during their first two dances, even after she'd corrected him. He hadn't let her get a word in edgewise, either, talking about playing cricket each time she saw him. Her parents wished for her to *marry* him?

Her stomach turned over, her brain woozy. This could not be happening. And why was her mother so anxious to be rid of her?

Her father continued. "Perhaps we should let her finish this season and find her a husband next year."

"Absolutely not. I want her married as quickly as possible—and it hardly matters to whom. I will speak to Sundridge's father myself, if necessary."

"No, no," her father said. "I'll see it handled, though I cannot understand why you are in such a hurry."

"It's best for Violet. Prolonging a betrothal won't help her prospects. A second season will only make everyone wonder what's wrong with her."

"There's nothing wrong with her with the girl. A bit shy, is all."

"Because you've indulged her. Our duty is to see her married now that she is of age. You promised, Charles. Have a betrothal in place before the month is out."

Violet put a hand on the wall to steady herself. Before the month was out? That was little more than a week from now. Was her mother serious?

She hurried away, moving swiftly along the corridor, her ears ringing with impending disaster. She had no destination in mind, only the need to keep going, to put distance between herself and this information.

Her mother wanted Violet gone. Married off to whomever would have her.

What sort of mother had no regard for the match her daughter made? Charlotte's mother hovered at her daughter's side, ensuring Charlotte only spoke with bachelors from the very best families. Violet's mother, on the other hand, hadn't attended large social events in months and anticipated ridding herself of her only child.

Tears burned Violet's lids as she moved toward the front door, the desire to escape overwhelming her. Their butler appeared, and his brow lowered in concern when he saw her face. "Did you wish to go out, Lady Violet?"

"I'd like to take a walk and visit my friend Charlotte."

"Of course, my lady. Shall I send for your maid?"

"No need. I am not going anywhere but to Charlotte's and it's not far."

"Then allow me to fetch a groom—"

Instead of waiting, Violet opened the door and dashed down the front walk. When she was far enough from her house, she hailed a hansom to take her to the far side of Grosvenor Square.

To Ravensthorpe.

She needed him to comfort her, to tell her it would be all right.

Even if it was a lie.

Max's large home sat on the corner of the very public square. Considering it was the middle of the day, she could not pay a call on him. Instead, she instructed the driver to let her out a block over and she then snuck into the rear of Max's gardens.

Tears streamed down her face as she hurried along. Thankfully, the gardeners were on the far side of the property, their backs to the house. After slipping onto the terrace and through the French doors, Violet ran along the corridor, hoping to avoid detection by the staff on her way to Max's study, where she assumed he was working.

Not bothering to knock, she turned the knob on the study door and slid in. Max was seated behind his desk, a young man scribbling on paper in the chair across from him. The duke's head snapped up, dark blue eyes locking on her face—and his jaw dropped. She hadn't a clue as what to do now that she was here, so she waited, silent tears rolling down her cheeks.

Max recovered quickly, coming to his feet. "Webber, let's pick this up later. You have enough to get started."

The other man gathered his things and bowed. "Your Grace."

Violet moved aside to let the young man pass. When they were alone, she tried to catch her breath, but emotion clogged her throat. Max came toward her, concern etched on his handsome features. "Violet, what is it? What's happened?"

Without waiting another second, she threw herself at his solid chest. He caught her, his arms holding her tight to his frame, and she breathed in his now-familiar scent of orange and tobacco. He was strong and safe, a balm for her misery. After a few seconds, her tears dried on his necktie, her shudders ceasing. When he picked her up, she clutched at his shoulders and buried her face in his throat.

He lowered them into a chair near the empty grate. The moment stretched and he seemed in no hurry to make her talk. For some reason, his calm fortitude helped soothe her. Finally, she sighed. "I'm sorry. I shouldn't have burst into your home in the middle of the day."

"I don't mind, though I do hope you came in the back."

"I did. No one saw me except the man who was here a moment ago."

"Webber is discreet. His job depends on it. Now, are you ready to tell me what is wrong, or shall I give you a present?"

She leaned back to see his face. "You bought me a present?"

The duke appeared adorably embarrassed, with his cheeks turning pink. "Yes, I did," he said. "Shocking, but I am capable of simple kindness, Violet."

This was more than simple kindness. This was . . . monumental. He'd bought her a *gift*.

He cares for me.

Her spirits lifted immediately—a considerable feat, seeing as how she was to be betrothed by the end of the month.

Max slid out from underneath her and went to his desk. When he came back, he was holding a rectangle-shaped box wrapped in brown paper. "I hope you like it."

Was he serious? The box could contain rocks and she would treasure them always. She tore through the paper with all the restraint of a three-year-old on Boxing Day. She gasped. "You bought me a camera."

Max thrust his hands in his trouser pockets and gave her a half smile. "I did."

"I've wanted a box camera for months. How did you know?"

"I had no idea. The clerk at the store recommended it."

She stood and placed the camera on the chair, then wrapped her arms around his middle. "Thank you, Max. It's the perfect gift. I love it."

He squeezed her tighter. "You're welcome."

They stood there for a long moment, locked in an embrace, and Violet thought she'd died and gone to heaven. Her problems felt far away while in the warm security of Max's arms. "Why does my mother hate me?"

Max's lips touched the crown of her head. "Come sit." He led her to an empty chair and pulled her onto his lap once again. "Why do you believe your mother hates you?"

She relayed the conversation she'd overhead. "She wants me betrothed by the end of the month."

"Perhaps it is as she said, that she is worried a second season will harm your chances."

"Do you believe that to be the case?"

"No. However, I haven't any daughters and I only married to produce an heir, so I am hardly an expert."

He so rarely spoke of his late wife and his son. She was curious about them, about anything regarding his life. "Tell me about her."

"Who?"

"Your wife."

He started, his body jerking slightly. "Why?"

"Because I'd like to know her."

* * *

MAX DIDN'T KNOW what to say. Part of him wished to refuse. He hated talking about Rebecca, and Will had long stopped asking about his mother. Those were memories best not stirred.

But perhaps Violet needed to understand. Marriages in their world were not for love or happiness. They were for progeny and legacy, to transfer wealth and property. Moreover, she needed to know of his past and why he'd never marry again.

He cleared his throat. "I decided to marry when I was twenty-four. I'd wrangled the accounts into some semblance of order and made several wise investments on the Exchange. There was no reason to wait."

He'd been the last of his friends to marry. Charles had settled down two years prior and Violet had already turned one. There was no need to mention it, however. Doing so would only make him feel like an old lecher, and this moment was about comforting her.

"Rebecca was pretty, the daughter of an earl. Her father had a large farm in Scotland with some sheep that I envied. He offered it as part of her dowry and I accepted." He'd sold the farm ages ago, as it had only served as a bitter reminder of his failure.

He stroked Violet's leg through her skirts. Thankfully, she'd stopped crying—a sight that had shredded his heart—and seemed to be breathing easier. He liked having her here, even during the day. Returning to his tale, he said, "I had thought we were a good match, that we'd muddle through together, but Rebecca was scared most all the time. Scared of acting improperly, scared of the staff gossiping. Scared of me."

"Scared of you?" She leaned back to see his face. "That is ridiculous. I've always thought you quite kind and generous."

He shook his head. Sweet girl. "I mean in the bedroom. She could not stand for me to touch her."

"Oh." Violet's nose wrinkled in the most adorable way. "I see."

"She knew her duty, of course. She allowed me to visit to her room at night, take her only under the covers and in the dark. Never undressed. I suspect she gritted her teeth through the whole business, despite my concerted efforts to ensure she enjoyed it. But the harder I tried, the more miserable she became."

"Perhaps she found the pleasure shameful."

It had crossed his mind, but he'd never learn the truth, unfortunately. "Perhaps. She wouldn't discuss it, though, and when she began increasing, I assumed we were both relieved." He had been so happy, so eager to be a father. To nurture and love a child as he hadn't been by his own father.

"Assumed? You mean she wasn't happy about carrying your child?"

"No, about sleeping with her. I assumed she'd gladly see me go elsewhere for my physical needs. That I could fuck whoever I wanted, seeing as how she didn't want me."

She frowned, her nose wrinkling. "A mistress."

He sighed, wishing he didn't have to tell Violet of his sordid past. *She'll never look at me the same.*

Perhaps it was for the best.

He carried on. "There was a woman from before my marriage. She was the wife of a viscount and we got on well together. I thought . . . I thought I was doing the right thing."

"It was insensitive of you, but you would not be the first married man in the ton to take a mistress."

"I realize as much, but as time went on I didn't try to hide it, either. Call it hubris or the idiocy of a twenty-five-year-old duke. I started staying away for longer stretches of time. Then I took my mistress to Rome—despite her husband's objections." He'd felt invincible, a man who had everything that mattered: wealth, a child on the way, and a beautiful woman at his side. He was cocksure and fearless, certain he knew best. "Rebecca was eight months along when the viscount wrote to her, informing her of what I'd done."

Violet began rubbing his chest, as if to soothe him—him, the man responsible for it all—and something inside Max shifted, unlocked. No one had comforted him in quite a while. He hadn't wanted it, frankly. But it was different with Violet. She eased his troubled soul, smoothed some of the jagged edges that scraped and cut inside him.

Clutching her tighter, he finished it. "There was no denying the viscount's claims, as I'd just returned days earlier. The news sent Rebecca into hysterics. She was inconsolable, crying and refusing to eat. She resented that I'd taken a mistress while she was carrying our child and considered it a betrayal of our marriage vows. Because of the unrest, the baby came early. I had the very best doctors at her side, but they couldn't save her."

"They were able to save the baby."

"Yes. Will was small, but he lived." His son had been so tiny, so fragile. But Will had fought to survive and Max had done everything in his power to see that his baby thrived. He had wet nurses around the clock and an army of nannies to keep a vigilant eye over the future duke. Max hardly left his son's side during that time.

"Max, you don't know whether she would have survived or not. Many happily married women die in childbirth."

He pressed his lips to her hair. "There's no need to lie. I was responsible for her death." That shame would follow him to his grave. "Which is why I will never marry again. I have no intention of subjecting another woman to that life."

"What life?"

"With me, failing at faithfulness."

"Max, you were so young."

"Older than you. Old enough to know better."

"Perhaps you wouldn't be unfaithful next time."

The hopeful note in her voice caused his tone to harden. "There will be no next time, Violet. I have no need to tie myself down when I already have an heir." He was not interested in ruining another woman he'd promised to honor and cherish. Max wouldn't risk it. A second dose of guilt would bury him.

"What about love? What about companionship?"

He hated to shatter her illusions, but it had to be said. "My dear, I've no need of the first and can find the second anytime I wish."

She was quiet after that, but he didn't take it back. Someone must give her the unvarnished truth. Someone must lower her expectations, both with regards to him and her future marriage.

A marriage not so far in the future, it seemed. Max hadn't a clue as to why Lady Mayhew was in a rush to marry Violet off, especially to a twit like Sundridge. Lady Mayhew hadn't ever seemed cruel, but perhaps the resentment in the Mayhew marriage had bled into her relationship with her daughter.

Still, Sundridge and Violet, married? Max's gut cramped at the thought. That fool did not deserve someone with Violet's spark or adventurous spirit. To hear her moans or capture her sighs with his mouth. To suck on her gorgeous tits or tongue her luscious cunt. It was out of the question.

"I'll have a word with Sundridge," he said curtly.

"Why?"

"Because you don't want to marry him."

"You say that as if they won't merely find someone else, another hapless soul to take Sundridge's place."

He didn't care much for that, either. "I won't let you marry just anyone. I'll use my influence to help you make the best possible match."

"Such as?"

"There's . . ." Every name that went through his head was instantly discarded. No man he knew was good enough for her. "Hmm."

She studied his face, observing his indecision like a hawk searching for prey. "Well?"

"I shall need to think on it."

She snuggled into his side and buried her nose in his neck. "I cannot see why I must marry at all. I could move into a small apartment in Chelsea above a camera shop, then maybe open my own photography studio."

And leave herself open to all sorts of mashers, charlatans, and miscreants? He sat straighter. "Absolutely not. That would hardly be safe."

"Perhaps, but I would be independent. I'd be willing to trade some peace of mind for that."

"I wouldn't."

"And I could still see you."

Satisfaction raced through him as he considered it—and he was instantly ashamed. Violet could not become his mistress. To do so would ruin her social standing and likely get Max shot by her father. "You do not want that life, darling. You deserve the protection and security of a proper marriage. To be pampered and provided for until you die."

"By a man like Sundridge? No, thank you." Clever fingers played along Max's jaw, stroking the skin above his collar. "Will you grant me a favor, Maximilian Thomas William Bradley III?"

His lips twisted into an affectionate smile. "Indeed, someone has been studying Debrett's."

"I used to write it on paper when I was younger."

Surprised, he leaned back to lock eyes with her. "You did?"

"Yes, and I drew little hearts around it, too."

He dropped his head onto the chair back. "Violet, my God. I should toss you in a carriage and send you home." But he wouldn't. Good sense had departed ages ago when it came to this woman. He couldn't get enough of her.

He'd never felt this connection with a lover before, this consuming need to not only touch and kiss her, but to just be with her, to talk about everything and nothing. Maybe it was because he'd known her for so long. Or perhaps it was merely Violet, this daring and intelligent woman who challenged him at every turn.

She playfully pushed his chest. "Stop talking nonsense. Will you grant me a favor or not?"

He tapped his fingers on the armrest, thinking. He didn't like agreeing without all the terms. However, this was Violet. History had shown that he had a difficult time telling her no, unless the topic was marriage.

He kissed her temple. "It depends."

"On?"

"On whether this request involves a lack of clothing and a flat surface."

"As a matter of fact, it does. Would you like to hear what I want?"

Blood gathered in his groin as he considered all the ways he planned to defile her this afternoon. "Of course. Name it and it's yours."

"May I photograph you?"

He blinked. "But I thought you said . . .?"

"Oh, I did." She cocked her head, her eyes dancing. "I want to photograph you without your clothes."

CHAPTER 8

When Max chuckled, Violet did not join in. The request hadn't been a jest. Devastatingly handsome, the duke was a specimen of living, breathing art, and if he did not deserve to be photographed and preserved, then nothing did.

He angled to see her face, the light catching on the threads of silver in his ink-colored hair. Her lower half clenched at his beauty, so harsh and masculine it hurt to look at him. His dark gaze narrowed on her. "Why?"

"Why not?"

"That is hardly an answer."

She smoothed the fabric covering his chest, petting him. "Because you are so very pretty and I wish to try out my new camera."

"Violet . . ."

He sounded exasperated, so she explained. "It's not uncommon. Shops near the Strand sell all sorts of—"

"You should not know of those places," he said sharply.

"Everyone knows of those places, Max."

"Do not wander in there. If you wish to see those types of images, I'll purchase them for you."

"Why not pose for them instead?"

"Back to this, are we?" He shook his head. "Not the sort of portrait a duke poses for, darling."

The endearment warmed her insides, but she didn't stop pressing him. "Please? The light is gorgeous right now, with the perfect amount of afternoon sun. We'll lock the door and the photos will only be for me, I promise."

"Until you are angry with me and then copies are shipped off to my enemies."

That stung. "Do you honestly believe I would ever do such a thing?"

"No, but they could end up in the wrong hands. What if your mother or father discovered them?"

She sensed victory. "My darkroom is in the attic and they never go up there."

"And you'll lock them up?" He pinched the bridge of his nose with a thumb and forefinger. "I cannot believe I am contemplating this. My ducal ancestors are undoubtedly spinning in their collective graves."

"What if you turn your head, so the camera cannot clearly see your face?"

"That sounds better, but only if you allow me to take some of you as well."

"Nude photographs?"

"Yes."

She licked her lips and shifted on his lap. Did she dare? He would see all her imperfections and flaws, captured for eternity.

"Not so brave now, are you?"

The taunt hit home, making her feel foolish. "Fine. I will if you will."

He ran a hand along her side and cupped her breast. "As long as I am able to keep the photographs of you."

She arched her back, pushing into his palm. "What will you do with them?"

"Stare at them while I stroke my cock."

The place between her legs pulsed at the idea. "Perhaps I'll do the same with your photographs."

"You mean use them whilst you masturbate? Oh, my sweet girl, nothing would bring me more joy."

Before she melted into a pool of lust on his plush carpets, she got up and readied the box camera. Max locked the door and then disrobed garment by garment until he was naked, his long and powerful body making her mouth water. On display were wide shoulders and a strong chest dusted with dark hair that trailed south, toward his flat belly. His penis was half-erect, the crown peeking out from the foreskin, with dark veins running along the shaft. And his muscled thighs were—

"If you keep staring at me like that, we'll never get around to actually taking the photographs."

She shook herself and tried to adopt a more professional demeanor. "Let's move the divan to maximize the light."

He helped her arrange the furniture to her liking, and then she told him to lie down. "Stretch out so the camera sees all those glorious angles and ridges."

"I had no idea you were so enamored by my looks. You are embarrassingly good for my vanity."

Please. Every woman in London salivated over him, as he well knew. "Put your arm behind your head and lean back."

He did as she asked, taking direction as she arranged him the way she wished. Goodness, he was delicious, as perfect as any museum sculpture. The sun cast him in an otherworldly glow, though certainly not angelic. More like a sinful treat on a hot summer's day, wicked and irresistible. The path to ruin, one she would choose time and time again.

Crouching, she took the first photo from an upward angle, where she could see his body but not his face. "Good. Just breathe and hold still."

The box camera was easy to hold and manipulate, and she was able to get close on his bicep, his rib cage. The whiskers on his jaw. He was quiet, letting her work, the sound of the camera doing all her talking. She couldn't wait to develop the full-length photos, the ones with his face in shadow while the rest of him was on splendid display, including his rapidly hardening cock.

He was relaxed grace and banked power, and she struggled to breathe. Her skin was hot and itchy, the throb between her legs growing more insistent. A fine sheen of sweat broke out on her forehead, like a fever had taken up residence inside her veins and the only cure was to lick him from head to toe.

Ahem.

"Now roll the other way."

He cocked a brow. "You want a photograph of my bare arse, then?"

Her face flamed but she didn't shrink from the request. "Seems a shame to waste the opportunity."

Max presented her with his back, his muscles shifting as he settled. She quickly pressed the button to capture the shot and turned the key to advance the film, even before he finished moving. The impulse to save every bit of him, forever, burned through her. Who knew how long she'd have the privilege of seeing him unclothed? If her parents had their wish, she'd be betrothed to another man by the end of the month.

Ignoring the heaviness in her chest at the thought, she kept working to find the perfect image of him, her legs dipping and bending, stepping closer, then farther away, while the minutes advanced.

Finally, Max's hand drifted between his legs. "I cannot stand this any longer. The more you look at me the more I want you. Are you finished?"

She nodded, her mouth dry. He'd rendered her speechless.

"Violet?" He peeked over his shoulder. When she didn't speak, he offered up a smooth grin. "Oh, I see. Enjoying yourself, are you? Perhaps I might offer assistance."

The film had run out, so she carefully placed the camera on a side table. "Thank you for humoring me."

Now flat on his back, he continued to stroke his large erection. "Are you wet, my little mouse?"

She watched the slow movements of his hand, mesmerized as he pulled and dragged, the muscles in his forearms popping. "I wish I had more film," she murmured.

He chuckled. "Too bad you don't have a moving picture camera."

Oh, there was a fine idea. "Would you—?"

"Indeed, not. This is for your eyes only. Come here." She reached him in two steps, and he tilted his head to look at her, his stern expression full of lust. "Take off your clothes."

It took her longer to undress on her own than if she'd had his help, but soon she was down to her drawers, stockings, and shoes. Color stained Max's cheeks, his chest rising and falling rapidly with the force of his breaths as he stared. Deciding to tease him, she lifted her foot and placed it on his thigh, the heel of her boot digging into his flesh. He jerked, his pupils dilating until his irises were nearly black.

He grunted. "In the mood for a bit rough?"

She unbuckled her shoe and removed it. "Perhaps I wish to torture you."

"Then press harder," he said with a daring lift of his brow.

She brought her other foot up and leaned on him, slowly unfastening the buckle on her shoe. He sucked in a harsh breath, his body tensing. "Hurry with the rest of it and get up here."

She shed her stockings and drawers and started to stretch out next to him, but he grabbed her arm. "Sit on my thighs. Put your knees on either side of my legs."

Climbing up, she positioned herself, which left her sex completely exposed. It would have been mortifying if Max weren't focused on her like a starving man. "Like this?"

"Yes. Lean back and put your left hand on my shin, then use your right hand between your legs. Show me what you'll do when you develop the pictures you took this afternoon."

Oh.

He was ordering her to do . . . that. In front of him.

"Max . . ."

"You are gorgeous, Violet. Show me, please."

She bit her lip. He hadn't stopped pleasuring himself. Where was the harm if she did the same? No one would know except for him, and he wouldn't judge her. He never did.

"Go on," he urged, his voice a low rasp.

Arching, she steadied herself with a hand on his leg. The position thrust her breasts up, which Max must have enjoyed because his hand moved quicker. Emboldened, she slipped her fingers into her sex, dipping into the folds until she grazed her clitoris. Pleasure sizzled in her veins and she sucked in a sharp breath.

"Goddamn, that is beautiful. Keep going. Let me watch you."

Gathering her courage, she used the pads of her fingers to swirl and tease, the skin swollen and slippery, while the scent of arousal permeated the air. They observed one another, a shared and intimate experience with hardly any contact, and somehow that aroused her more. She tried to bedevil him, exaggerating her movements, thoroughly enjoying herself while her body climbed toward its peak. Max panted and cursed, his muscles straining as he pumped his fist, and his reaction spurred her on.

At some point, Max released his erection and placed his hands on her thighs, a light sheen of sweat coating his entire body. His penis was a dull red and fully engorged, resting on his stomach, waiting to be put to good use. And she wanted it. There was an emptiness inside her, an ache, and there would never be another man in her life like this one. Not like Max.

The time was right. She knew it in her bones.

"Max, I want another favor."

His gaze remained focused on the place between her legs. "Anything, darling."

"Will you be my first?"

He froze, his eyes locking with hers while his fingers dug into her thighs. "Your first time should be with your future husband. Not me. I cannot marry you."

Lord, she was tiring of hearing him say that.

She pressed harder on the taut bud and her eyes nearly rolled back in her head. "Why should I wait . . . to bestow this honor . . . on a nameless and faceless future husband?"

He licked his lips, his expression turning decidedly predatory. Like he was imagining all he wished to do to her. Streaks of white-hot pleasure rolled along her spine.

"You want me to ruin you." His voice was rough, with sharp edges and unyielding authority. He could command an army with that tone. God knew she'd do anything he asked when he spoke to her like that.

"Yes, I do." Then she landed a blow of her own. "Please, *Your Grace*."

As if on cue, his right eye twitched. "You'll regret it."

Impossible. She'd dreamed of this for so long, and he had exceeded her imaginings, the elaborate fantasies she'd concocted in her head over the years. The real man was infinitely more alluring, more caring, and there was no reason to hold back. She wanted to drown in him, to lose herself in his breath and surrender to his caresses. "No, I won't."

"Stand up."

She crawled off his lap and stood on the floor. Max rose and towered over her. "You still wish to do this? You want me to fuck you?"

"Yes."

"You are going to be the death of me. Let's go." Not bothering with clothes, he took a hold of her wrist and led her to the back corner of the study. Where were they going?

He pushed a section of the wainscoting, and the wall popped open.

"A secret passage?" How thrilling.

"Go." He ushered her into the darkness, then flicked a switch that illuminated a single bulb. A set of stairs waited to the left. "Climb."

She ascended the stairs, Max right behind her. She could sense him, large and looming, and her skin crackled with awareness, every cell vibrating with readiness. Was this truly happening?

At the top of the stairs, he reached to open a latch, then pushed on the wood. Beyond, a bedchamber was revealed. *His bedchamber.*

Her heart pounded, a steady thrumming of disbelief that she was finally here after so many years of dreaming about it. It was like she'd been invited into Heaven—or more like Hell. This was Ravensthorpe, after all.

She walked inside, her wide gaze taking it all in. A huge dark walnut bed dominated the space, while an armoire, side table, and single leather chair comprised the remaining furniture. Sparse artwork on the walls. As decadence went, the space left quite a lot to be desired. Standing by the bed, she dragged her fingertips over his simple bedclothes. "Hmm."

"You sound disappointed." He closed the panel in the wall. "What were you expecting?"

"Velvet and gilding, I think. A list of men you're exacting revenge upon. Perhaps a special coitus chair, like the one the Prince of Wales supposedly owns in France."

He made a choking sound, his eyes bulging. "How on earth do you know about that chair?"

"Have you seen it?" His lips flattened, and she had her answer. "Tell me. I overheard ladies discussing it in Paris at a ball."

"I will not. And I'd rather discuss you than Bertie. Are you certain about this? You may change your mind at any time, you know."

Even though she was feeling shy and longing for a dressing gown, Violet had never been more certain of anything in her life. "I want this. I want *you.*"

He pulled her close with one arm and used his free hand to roll her nipple between his thumb and forefinger. "Have I told you how much I adore your breasts?"

"You do?"

"Very much so. I would love to pierce these gorgeous nipples with jewelry. Did you hear of that when you were in Paris?"

That was something people did? "No." She watched his hand, her breath stuttering as his thick fingers pulled and massaged the tip of her breast. Each movement sent spikes of pleasure straight between her legs.

"It's in fashion these days. Rings that hang from the breast, sparkling with gems. I could tug on them gently, give you a tiny bite of pain. Would that be rough enough for you?"

"I think I might like that," she said, feeling dazed, drunk on his presence. Yet his talk of the future penetrated the fog in her brain. "So, does this mean we'll continue to see each other?"

* * *

CLEVER GIRL. Max should have known she'd pick up on that. "For now, let's focus on your request, shall we?"

She reached to stroke his shaft. "Just tell me what to do."

Max groaned and struggled for composure. He knew this was a mistake. He had no right to take her virginity, but he was past the point of talking her out of it. She was a grown woman and if this was what she wanted, then who was he to deny her?

His erection was so painful, he had to grit his teeth. Twice he'd nearly orgasmed while watching her pleasure herself and if he didn't spend soon, his balls might explode.

Still, he had to make this good for her.

He stilled her hand and gestured to the bed. "Lie back on the mattress."

The bed was the perfect height for him to feast on her cunt, and he wasted no time in doing so as soon as she was in position. He kissed and licked her, leaving no bit of skin untended between her legs. He even brushed his tongue over the puckered rose of her bottom, which caused her to gasp, and he made a mental note to return to that area someday soon. *Oh, the pleasures I will give you, my little mouse.*

"Max, please," she begged, her thighs trembling aside his head. "Your Grace. Oh, please."

He couldn't resist her when she begged in that tone, so he tongued her clitoris, suckling while sliding his index finger inside her. Her walls gripped his skin, reminding him of the narrow width of her opening. *You cannot hurt her.*

On his wedding night, he had tried to prepare Rebecca, but she'd wanted the whole business done quickly. Max had assumed his wife's reticence had been nerves during her first time, but it soon became clear Rebecca didn't enjoy their coupling. At all. No amount of preparation had pleased her.

He had to do better by Violet.

Her hips soon met the pumping of his hand, his finger slipping easily into her quim, so he added another. Violet's fingertips curled into the bedclothes, fabric bunching in her palms as she mewled in her throat, her body undulating toward its peak. "Oh, God."

By the time he used three fingers, she was drawn tight, shaking with need. Then the taut bud swelled and tightened in his mouth and she broke, her walls clenching around his fingers, milking them, and Max nearly came on the floor. Goddamn, he could not wait to be inside her.

Rising, he climbed onto the bed and slid between her thighs. "Lift your knees."

She obeyed without question, spreading herself open, her sex flushed from her orgasm, the skin glistening with her slickness. Had he ever seen anything more arousing in his life? Gripping the base of his cock, he lined up at her entrance then paused. His chest heaved as desire clawed inside him like a rabid beast, desperation a fever in his blood. "Are you certain?"

She widened her thighs even further and Max's brain turned to porridge. He pushed forward ever so slightly, working the head of his cock inside her tight sheath. The walls squeezed him like a fist, and he had to close his eyes, breathe deeply, to keep from rutting at her like an animal.

"Oh," Violet said.

He lifted his head and studied her. Violet's eyes were wide, as if she was surprised. "Are you in pain? Discomfort?" Rebecca had cried their first time, her tears soaking their bed. "Shall I stop?"

She shook her head. "Do not dare."

He exhaled, relief and affection settling in his chest, lightening his mood. Vowing to go slow, he moved carefully, steadily, watching her the entire time for signs of distress. She was breathing heavily, her skin flushed, as he slid into her body. It was bloody torture, with streaks of lust crackling along the backs of his thighs, his cock demanding friction.

When he bottomed out, he held there, motionless, sucking in air as he gave her time to adjust. Being inside her was heaven, a tight, wet paradise that he never wanted to leave. Violet was all he could see, all he could feel, and he wished he could stay right here, like this, for the rest of the day and into the night.

Soon he couldn't wait any longer. "All right?" he asked through clenched teeth.

"I expected to be torn in two. Instead I feel . . . full." She wriggled, causing him to shift inside her, and he screwed his eyes shut, struggling not to spend before they even got started. "I like it," she said.

Dear God.

Max gave a thrust of his hips, his shaft dragging along her sensitive tissues, and Violet purred. "Goodness, I like that even more."

He was done for.

Any civility he possessed disappeared and Max snapped, driving into her again and again. At some point she dropped her knees and clutched at him, pulling him closer as he fucked her like a man possessed. Her body slid higher on the mattress and he chased her, unwilling to let her get away even for a moment. A part of him knew he was being too rough, too barbaric for her first time. But she only moaned and scored his skin with her nails, telling him in breathy pants, "more" and "faster."

The woman would be his undoing.

He leaned over her, snarling in her ear as his hips worked, his cock plunging in and out of her channel. "You like this, my little mouse? You want more?"

"Oh, Max, yes. Please."

"You're going to let me fuck you whenever I want, aren't you?" He couldn't seem to stop talking, especially when her walls clenched every time he did. *She likes my dirty words.* "Your cunt was made for my cock. I've never had better."

It was the truth. But he knew it wasn't her body—it was *her*.
You're falling for her.

Unwilling to give credence to such ridiculousness, he shut off his brain and thrust hard. Then he used his thumb on her clitoris, stimulating the button until Violet's back began to bow, her breasts bouncing as continued to work himself in and out of her. Finally, she arched, crying out as her walls contracted around his cock. Flashes of heat streaked along Max's spine, through his bollocks, but he somehow held out while watching her orgasm, the sight more alluring than anything he'd ever witnessed.

As soon as she started to relax, it was tempting to let his body take over, surrender to the bliss that rocketed through his system. Yet he couldn't finish inside her. Quickly, he pulled out and crawled up her body, his knees astride her chest, and aimed the tip of his shaft at her mouth. "Open," he growled.

She parted her lips and he drove between them, groaning as her tongue swirled on the underside of his shaft as if coaxing his spend. Then it happened. The orgasm roared through him, sensation shooting along his thighs and out the tip of his cock. It went on and on, wave after glorious wave of euphoria, his muscles trembling as he gave her everything he had.

He slumped, nearly falling over, weak as a kitten in the aftermath. Violet continued to lick his shaft, her mouth gentle, and stared up at him with such adoration and satisfaction that his lips twisted into a half grin. He hadn't smiled this much in . . . ages. But Violet had that effect on him. In the short time they'd been lovers, he found himself thinking of her at the oddest moments, with small comments he wished to tell her, as if she'd invaded his brain with her sweet and earnest nature.

Running his hand through her disheveled hair, he almost blurted out a very stupid sentence.

You cannot ruin this girl's life. Begging her to be your mistress is selfish, Max.

God, but he wanted her. Day and night. Ready at his disposal, with her easy smile and keen observations, not to mention her delectable body.

He dropped onto his back and tried to catch his breath. Violet rolled closer, snuggling into his side, and he wrapped his arm around her.

"You are very good at that," she said, her head resting on his shoulder. "No wonder your mistresses fight to keep you."

It had never been like this, but he didn't tell her that. "I am pleased you enjoyed yourself. I haven't much experience with virginity." Only his late wife, and no one would deem that a success.

"Max, it was perfect." She pressed a kiss to his skin. "Just as I knew it would be with you."

He shifted to cradle her cheek in his palm. "I should be reassuring you. Did I hurt you?"

"No." She bit her lip and wiggled slightly. "I am a bit sore, but I cannot wait to do that again."

A chuckle escaped Max's throat. "What am I to do with you, my sweet girl?"

"I am certain you'll think of something, Your Grace."

CHAPTER 9

*V*iolet forced a smile at her dance partner. What on earth made her parents believe Lord Sundridge a good choice for a husband? While he wasn't particularly hard on the eyes, he talked nonstop. She'd stopped listening ages ago, instead memorizing three rote comments to interject whenever he paused for a reaction: "Indeed, I daresay you are right," "How clever of you," and "One can never know, I suppose."

Thus far, he hadn't seemed to notice that her mind was elsewhere. Or, rather on *someone*.

Max stood on the far side of the room, towering over the other men in his perfectly tailored evening clothes. His dark hair was expertly styled, his expression bored to the casual observer. Violet knew better, however.

The Duke of Ravensthorpe was watching her every move.

Oh, he might not have stared directly at her, but he observed carefully, keeping to her vicinity, and his keen gaze brushed over her person no matter where she was in the room.

She could swoon with the possessiveness of it. The duke, possessive of *her*. Her core squeezed in happiness, despite the soreness from yesterday. Though she and Max would never marry, she would never regret giving him her virginity. The experience had been utterly divine, satisfying in every way.

Which left her the problem of Sundridge. Her current dance partner was carrying on a one-sided conversation that seemed more like a lecture aimed at no one in particular. Above all else, she could not marry this man.

Had her father already spoken to Sundridge's father? Dread slithered over Violet's skin, turning her stomach. Why was her mother anxious to marry her off, even to a nincompoop? It made no sense.

Perhaps she should try and reason with Sundridge.

"My lord," she said, interrupting whatever he'd been saying.

Sundridge blinked at her. "Don't care for cricket, do you?"

Was that the topic on which he'd been rambling? "Our dance will end soon, and I wished to ask a question before we part."

"Oh. Has this to do with cricket?"

"No, actually." God help her. "It has to do with us. Are you . . . that is, our fathers . . ."

"Yes?" He had the nerve to sound impatient.

"Are you considering marriage? To me, I mean?" Two months ago, this conversation would have mortified her. Now, too much hung in the balance not to address it.

"I . . . yes. I thought my intent was quite clear."

"Why?"

"Why is it clear?"

"No, why me?"

He cleared his throat. "Well, why not?"

Hardly a statement of ever-loving devotion. "I cannot see that we have anything in common."

"You shall come to like cricket, Lady Violet, I swear."

"It's more than that. We hardly know one another." She lowered her voice. "Wouldn't you rather marry a girl with whom you are somewhat familiar?"

He gave her a look that suggested she belonged in an insane asylum. "You seem like a nice, quiet girl, docile. I think we'll get on just fine."

He made her sound like a cow. Her back straightened, anger burning her throat. "I am hardly quiet. I have opinions and thoughts of my own, which I cannot verbalize because you never cease talking!"

Heads around them swiveled. The other dancers looked shocked at the outburst, and she pressed her lips together, chagrined . . . but not apologetic.

Indeed, this was not the time or place for such a conversation, though she did intend to dissuade him from offering for her. Soon.

"Excuse me, my lord." Offering a quick curtsy, she dashed off the dance floor and headed toward the terrace doors. She kept her head down and hoped Max wouldn't see her. She needed solitude at the moment, not Max's insistence that all marriages were miserable or—God forbid—another offer to help find her a husband. How would she survive it if the only man she'd ever wanted arranged to wed her off to someone else?

Violet would rather die.

And what happened if she could not get out of a marriage to Sundridge?

A light mist fell onto the empty terrace, the dreary type of precipitation London served in a never-ending supply. Violet didn't mind the water. It felt cool on her overheated skin, a balm for the rawness in her chest. Was this her destiny? To marry a man she didn't want and relive memories of Max for the rest of her life?

She tilted her face to the sky and let the rain mix with the tears building on her lashes.

What am I to do with you, my sweet girl?

His words haunted her, even hours later. *Love me,* she'd wanted to tell him. *Never let me go.* But she knew what he would have said in response . . . and it would have broken her heart.

Can I do this?

Could she love a man who would never claim her publicly? Who would rather keep her hidden away in the darkness? Violet had once thought it wouldn't bother her, that she would do anything the Duke of Ravensthorpe asked.

But it *hurt*. Far more than she'd ever expected. She didn't want to hide or pretend. She longed to be at his side, in the daylight. Bear his children. *Be his wife.*

That would never happen. He'd made it painfully clear from the start.

A sound near the door had her wiping her face. Was it Max? She didn't wish for him to find her crying out here.

"Lady Violet?"

Sundridge. Her shoulders sank.

Turning, she folded her arms and inclined her head. "My lord."

After casting an unhappy glance at the sky, he drew closer, stopping just within reach. His dark blond hair immediately lost its artful tousling thanks to the water droplets. "I sensed you were upset on the dance floor and I wanted to check on your welfare. And apologize, of course, for whatever I might have said to aid in your distress."

Perhaps Sundridge wasn't so bad after all. "Thank you. I shouldn't have raised the topic of marriage in such a public place, I suppose."

"I had assumed . . . Well, I assumed when I kept asking you to dance that you realized I was serious about courting you."

"Why me?"

"As I said, I've found nothing objectionable about you. I think we shall get on quite well together."

"Is it the dowry?" Violet was aware that her status as an heiress would entice nearly any man. *Save Max, of course.*

"We do need it," he said. "I cannot pretend otherwise. That is not my only reason for choosing you, however."

Do I not get a choice, as well? She wished to shout the question into the cool night air, but what good would it serve? The answer was obvious, and everyone knew it. Still, she had to try. "What if I told you my heart was promised to another?"

Sundridge lifted a bony shoulder. "I think we should focus on friendship and compatibility. A marriage is a partnership, sort of like a cricket team. You see—"

"What about happiness?"

"If you are asking if I'll tolerate pursuits outside of our marriage, I won't object. We'll need children, of course, but that's no hardship."

Violet wilted, unable to countenance what was happening. Her life was spinning out of control, her future full of nothing but misery and compromise.

Sundridge gripped her arm and moved closer. "May I call you Violet?" Without awaiting an answer, he said, "Violet, I realize how young girls romanticize these things, but this is a time for strategy. Like in cricket, you might give up something now to gain a run or two later."

What in God's name was he talking about? She tried to pull free, to no avail. "You aren't listening to me—"

A voice cracked through the night like the lash from a whip. *"Release her."*

The Duke of Ravensthorpe emerged from the gloom, looking like an avenging angel ready to lay waste to everything in his path. Violet's heart clenched as he stalked forward, his eyes burning into the younger man at her side. "I said to release her, Sundridge. *Now.*"

Sundridge held up his hands. "I—I didn't hurt her, I swear."

Max glanced at Violet. "Are you hurt, Lady Violet?"

"No, Your Grace." She didn't know what do. Why was Max here? Had he been worried about her? She bit her lip and tried to contain the urge to throw herself into his arms.

You're a secret. You'll always be just a secret.

Max rounded on the younger man. "You are lucky no one else caught you out here. Were you trying to ruin her reputation? I hadn't thought you such a bounder, Sundridge."

"I came to converse with her. That's all." Sundridge sidled away from Max, his skin going pale. "I never meant any disrespect."

Max advanced, his hands curling into fists. "I saw her try to pull away when you grabbed her. Are you telling me I am wrong?"

Sundridge's back met the balustrade. He was trapped. Max didn't stop, snatching Sundridge's throat in a strong hand and leaning in. The younger man pleaded, "Your Grace, I swear. It was innocent. We were only talking. Tell him, Lady Violet!"

"I know what I saw," Max snarled and shook Sundridge once. "I ought to punch you in the mouth for lying."

Sundridge's face started to turn purple and Violet panicked. She'd never seen Max this enraged, this out of control. Would he honestly harm Sundridge in the midst of a ball?

Rushing forward, she put her hand on Max's arm. "Max, stop. Let him go!"

Max released Sundridge's throat and the younger man began to cough in an effort to breathe. Not quite finished, Max jerked Sundridge by a lapel and tossed him in the direction of the terrace steps. "Go home, Sundridge. And if I ever see you near her again I'll make certain you regret it."

Sundridge didn't look back. He hurried down the stone steps and disappeared into the gardens, likely headed to the mews. Max smoothed his jacket and pulled on his cuffs. She frowned at him, shocked by his display of irrational behavior. "Have you lost your—"

"What in the bloody hell, Ravensthorpe?"

Spinning, she saw her father near the French doors—and he appeared livid.

* * *

THE RAGE-INDUCED fog began to recede from Max's brain, only to be replaced by dread. Violet's father stood on the terrace, his mouth flattened into a furious line. Just how much had Charles seen and heard?

Max decided to go with the easiest reaction, which was righteous imperviousness. "I was returning from the gardens, Mayhew, when I happened along Sundridge manhandling your daughter. I assumed you'd appreciate my lending her my protection to avoid a nasty scene."

Charles stalked forward, his dress shoes slapping on the wet stone. "You were not in the gardens, Ravensthorpe, because I saw you slip out the terrace doors a few moments ago. I followed because I wished to talk to you—and then I catch you nearly strangling a man to death and my daughter calling you Max." He pointed in Max's face. "So I'll ask again, what in the bloody hell is going on?"

Shit. Charles had seen and heard most all of it, apparently. Though his chest burned with regret, Max forced out a lie. "I am saving your daughter's reputation, obviously."

"Violet, return inside," Charles barked, not taking his eyes off Max.

"But Papa—"

"Now, Violet."

Max raised a brow, using calm logic to diffuse this disastrous situation. "She's soaked to the bone, Mayhew. You cannot order her inside the ballroom in her current state."

Charles's gaze, full of fury and resentment, narrowed on Max before shifting to his daughter. "Go around the side of the house and find our carriage. *Now.*"

Max had to bite his tongue to keep from admonishing his friend for the way he spoke to Violet, who had done absolutely nothing wrong in this instance. Instead, he clasped his hands behind his back and tried to wipe any trace of emotion off his face.

"No, Papa. If you are going to discuss me, then I have a right to stay."

"Absolutely not. Get to the carriage this instant, daughter." Charles did not waver and Violet licked her lips, uncertainty creeping into in her expression.

Finally, she addressed Max. "Thank you for coming when you did, Your Grace." Her voice wavered slightly, making him long to pick her up and hold her, but he merely nodded instead. In a swirl of wet silk, she disappeared down the terrace steps.

"I want to know what is going on between you and Violet," Charles snarled. "You will tell me this instant."

"Don't be ridiculous," Max drawled. "There is nothing going on."

Charles's lips twisted. "She called you Max. She put her hand on your arm. I saw the way she looked at you, unafraid and adoring. There is a familiarity there, one that hasn't existed before, and I want to know why, goddamn it."

Max clenched his jaw, his mind spinning on a plausible response . . . but came up empty.

"My God." With both hands, Charles shoved Max into the stone balustrade. Anger hardened his features into a mask of rage. "You bastard. Have you compromised my daughter?"

There was no hope for it. Charles had seen too much and they knew each other too well. Max braced himself. "Yell a little louder, Mayhew. I don't think they heard you in Cheapside."

"How could you? My *daughter*."

Charles stripped off his right glove and pulled his arm back. Max knew it was coming, so he waited, holding perfectly still, aware that he deserved it. The fist connected with his jaw, driving him into the stone railing once more. *Bloody hell, that hurt.* Max bent over and dragged in a breath, struggling through the pain. "That's the only one you'll get, Mayhew."

"You goddamn arsehole. My only child and you had to defile her. What, are there not enough women in London already for you? No doubt you've given Violet the clap, you prick—"

Max grabbed Mayhew and reversed their positions, shoving the other man against the stone before leaning in. "I do not have the clap—and watch your mouth."

"She's not much older than your son. You've known her since she was a baby."

Stepping back, Max swept the water off his face. "She is not a child anymore. She is a grown woman. Nevertheless, I did not plan this. It just happened."

"I never thought . . ." Charles shook his head. "You've never gone for the young ones before. I thought she was safe with you around."

"She *is* safe with me around," Max growled. "I would never hurt her."

"She was an innocent, Ravensthorpe. By touching her, you've harmed her."

"I am discreet. No one knows of our association."

"Except for Sundridge. And now me." Charles raked Max with a look full of disgust. "All these years you've been coming to my home, eating dinner with my family, and you've been lusting after her. I ought to put a bullet in your rotten heart."

Anger swept through Max at the indecent implication. He pointed a finger in Charles's face. "I never lusted after her until recently. This all happened within the last month."

"Christ." For a moment, Charles appeared like he might cry. Then he drew himself up. "Is she carrying your child?"

"Absolutely not."

"Are you entirely certain?"

Max paused, because how could one ever be entirely certain? "I am fairly certain."

He'd taken precautions over the years never to subject another woman to childbirth. The possibility of death was too great a risk, and the idea of Violet writhing in agony, bleeding to death because of his lust, sent a bolt of cold fear through his veins.

Charles slapped the stone with his palm. "Goddamn you, Ravensthorpe."

"Even still, I won't marry her."

Charles's jaw fell. "You think I want my daughter married to *you*?" He gave a bitter laugh. "You killed your first wife. Do you actually believe I'd give my sweet and trusting daughter over to the likes of you?"

Max folded his arms across his chest and worked to remain calm. It wasn't anything he hadn't told himself, but it stung to hear it out of his friend's mouth. "No, I suppose not. Fortunately, no one knows of my association with her. Sundridge will assume my friendship with you to be the reason I intervened tonight. Her reputation remains pristine."

Charles acted as if he hadn't heard a word Max said. "Now the rumors about you and Wingfield make sense. I heard you accosted him at Brooks's, but I hadn't believed it. That was over Violet, wasn't it?"

"Do not make this into something it isn't, Mayhew."

Charles dragged a hand through his wet hair. "I cannot believe, after all our years of friendship, that you would do this. That you could care so little for my family. That you could be so callously cruel."

The moment stretched, the steady drizzle of rain continuing to soak them both, but neither moved. An awful sensation swept across Max's skin and burrowed into his chest like talons—a sensation he suspected was guilt. However, no promises had been hinted at between him and Violet. He hadn't lied—she'd known his intentions at every turn. He hadn't whispered pretty words merely to get under her skirt. He hadn't needed to.

Still, he didn't relish exposing the affair and hurting her. Damn Mayhew for forcing him to do it.

It's for the best. She was never meant for me, anyway.

The world believed him vicious and selfish. A monster who drove his first wife into the grave. It was past time to prove it.

Drawing himself up to his most menacing height, he drawled, "You are overreacting. I haven't hurt her or ruined her chances at marriage with Sundridge. 'Tis a lark between us. Nothing more."

"It had better be, because I'm betrothing her to Sundridge, if he'll still have her. As for you, I hope you rot in hell, Ravensthorpe."

Charles shoved Max out of the way and headed for the steps. "Oh, and Ravensthorpe?" He glared at Max. "If I ever see you in the vicinity of my daughter again, death sentence or not, I'll shoot you right between the eyes."

Then he disappeared and Max was alone, the sound of the raindrops his only company. He stared at his shoes and tried not to drown in his regrets.

I did the right thing.

There had been no choice but to tell Charles. Violet wouldn't agree, certainly, but she'd thank Max one day after she married some young lord and had a passel of children. A cantankerous, cynical duke such as himself had no right to a vivacious and optimistic young woman like Violet. She had years of joy and discovery ahead of her, while he had long crested that particular hill.

He rubbed the center of his chest, where a dull ache had set up residence. Yes, it was definitely for the best.

CHAPTER 10

*V*iolet couldn't move, her back stuck to the stone as rain slithered into her bodice and behind her neck. Her stupid heart oozed misery, as if it had been sliced open to bleed out on the grass.

A lark. He'd called her a *lark*. Dismissed and diminished her.

That is what you get for eavesdropping.

Yet how was she expected to leave when her father and Max were discussing her? Of course, she had stayed—though a big part of her now wished she hadn't.

Chest tight, she lifted her face toward the sky, longing to start over again, back before she'd romanticized thoughts of a dark-headed duke with eyes like midnight.

It's better to know how little you mean to him.

She would never be more than a secret, a diversion he used to the pass the time. He would never love her, not as she loved him.

Indeed, she'd thought she could handle an affair, that having a piece of him was better than nothing at all. What foolishness. What hubris. Turned out it hurt to settle for scraps. She wanted every bit of Max, his body and his heart. His soul.

'Tis a lark between us. Nothing more.

Goodness, she couldn't breathe. She tapped her sternum with her fist, reminding her lungs to function. It must have worked because she was still standing when her father came storming down the stairs.

When he spotted her, he stopped. "I see you heard." Grimacing, he closed his eyes. "I would have spared you that, but I suppose it's best you learn what type of man he is."

Your cunt was made for my cock, Violet. I've never had better.

Even if he'd been telling the truth, their intimate moments had meant nothing to him. *She* had meant nothing to him.

Swallowing, she faced her father. "I'd like to go home."

"Come." He took her arm and towed her along in the rain. "God, Violet. I would have wished any other man in the entire world for you. He is the very last one—"

"Not now, Papa."

There must have been something in her voice, something desperate and broken, because he clamped his lips shut. They ended up in front of the house, and the Mayhew carriage was soon brought around. With the evening still in full swing, the streets remained quiet at this hour. Violet was grateful for the rain, as it washed away the tears leaking from her eyes.

When they were settled inside, her father handed her a dry cloth. Violet wiped her face slowly. "I am sorry, Papa."

"Sorry it happened—or sorry you were caught?"

She couldn't answer. The wound was too raw, her body still sore from Max's attentions yesterday.

Papa exhaled and pushed the wet hair off his forehead. "I am trying to remain calm, but it is a struggle. How on earth did this happen?"

She forced the admission past the lump holding court in her throat. "You mustn't blame Ravensthorpe. I threw myself at him—more than once, I might add—and he tried to warn me off many times. Also, he told me that he would never marry me."

"Then, why?"

"Because I've loved him ever since I was a girl."

And I thought I could make him love me, too.

"Your mother was right. I allowed you far too much independence with your camera and your classes. We should have kept you limited to traditional pursuits at home with a governess."

On the dark street were the familiar houses that lined their perfect little world, a society where young girls had no control over their future. Where parents used their daughters like bargaining chips. There was a great fascinating city out there, one she'd never experience or explore because it had been deemed unsafe for girls like her.

"We'll marry you off to Sundridge and no one ever need know," her father was saying.

"Papa, he could barely bother to learn my name and all he talks of is cricket."

"You act as if you have options at the moment, Violet. Allow me to dissuade you of that notion. Sundridge is your only hope."

A sob worked its way out of her chest, but she pushed it down. There would be time enough for that later. "I do not want to marry him."

"You could be increasing," Papa hissed, his eyes full of disappointment and anger. "Have you thought of that?"

Max hadn't spent inside her, so she doubted a child would result. Those details were not something she wished to discuss with her father, however. "Nevertheless, that is no reason to rush into a miserable marriage."

Papa leaned in. "I will not have my daughter bear a child out of wedlock."

The absolute nerve . . . Her lips curved into a knowing sneer as she leaned in as well. "You mean like the child you fathered with a mistress two years ago?"

One could have heard a pin drop in the carriage. He stared at her as if she'd smacked him. "How . . . how do you know of that? Did he tell you?"

"Ravensthorpe and I never once discussed the particulars of your reprehensible behavior. I heard the maids talking about it. The woman came to the house when Mama and I were away, apparently."

He dragged a hand down his jaw. "You mustn't tell your mother. She'd . . . well, she has a weak heart and I'm afraid the news might kill her."

More like he feared Mama might kill *him* if she found out.

"Then you'll not marry me off to Sundridge."

"Are you—are you *blackmailing* me, Violet?"

She hadn't planned on it, but she wouldn't take the words back. Resolve hardened inside her, a small sense of satisfaction that eased her misery. "It appears I am."

"What happens if you find yourself with child?"

"Then I'll go away. No one will know."

"Absolutely not. It's too great a risk. You must marry quickly, Violet. For this . . . and other reasons."

Because her mother wanted her gone.

She turned toward the window. "I will choose my husband."

After a long silence, her father said, "He won't marry you, even if you're carrying his child."

As if she didn't know that already. Tonight, Max's position regarding her had been made abundantly clear. She fought to hold back the tears burning behind her lids. "I am aware. I want nothing more to do with the Duke of Ravensthorpe."

"Well, I'm relieved to hear it. He has promised discretion and I believe he means it. We'll find another suitor soon. Dowry's too large to ignore for most of these gents."

Violet didn't speak. She had no intention of entertaining another suitor, ever.

"Most importantly," Papa said, "I will ensure he keeps far away from you."

Max wouldn't chase her. Why would he? There were other larks, women who wouldn't hope for more. Women who wouldn't develop feelings for him. Sophisticated and smart women like Louisa, satisfied with stolen moments and the occasional tryst.

But that was not Violet, not any longer.

* * *

A LETTER. He'd sent her a letter.

A week had gone by—the most miserable seven days of Violet's life—and now Max had sent her a letter. She stared at the paper warily, as if it might burst into flames at any moment.

Why had he bothered?

"Lady Violet? Are you all right?"

Shaking herself, Violet looked at the housemaid who had presented Max's secret communiqué. "Forgive me, Katie. You said a boy delivered this?"

Katie nodded. "Yes, milady. He appeared while I was picking herbs in the back. Told me to give it directly to you and no one else."

"Thank you. I trust I can rely on your discretion."

"Of course, milady. I promise not to tell a soul." Katie curtsied and departed, leaving Violet alone in her bedchamber.

She placed the missive on her bed and studied it. The letter was thin, just a single sheet of paper, with no writing on the outside. Max's familiar ducal signet ring had been pressed into the sealing wax.

Part of her wished to tear it open and devour every word.

The more rational side, however, feared additional heartbreak. Hadn't she suffered enough? Unless his letter contained words of undying devotion and a marriage proposal . . .

A bitter sound escaped her throat. Max? A marriage proposal? Ludicrous. He would never marry her and she would forever be his secret.

Her door flew open and Charlotte appeared. "Violet, you missed our appointment."

Violet lunged for the letter and tried to shove it under the pillow. Unfortunately, her friend wasn't fooled.

"Is that a letter you're trying to hide?"

"No," Violet lied. "We had an appointment today?"

"Shopping and tea, remember? I cannot believe you forgot." She pointed at the pillow. "Was that a letter from one of your suitors?"

"No, definitely not." The idea of Max courting her was laughable.

Charlotte folded her arms, a determined set to her chin. "Out with it. You forgot our outing, there are dark circles under your eyes, and now you have this letter. What is going on?"

Violet waivered. The strain of keeping all this heartbreak to herself for so many days weighed on her chest. Ever since the night of the ball, she'd swallowed her grief, pushed her misery down to where no one would notice, and it made her brittle. A fragile creature who might break at any moment.

Perhaps sharing a slice of her anguish might help.

"It is from a man, but not a suitor."

"The plot thickens." When Violet remained silent, Charlotte removed her hat and tossed it on the bed. "Are you planning to tell me who?"

Before she could reconsider the wisdom of a confession, Violet let the words out. "The Duke of Ravensthorpe."

Charlotte gasped and clutched a bedpost. "Ravensthorpe? Have you lost your mind?"

"Yes, apparently."

"But he's . . . old. Handsome, but old. And Violet," she dropped her voice, "they say he killed his first wife."

Though he'd broken her heart, Violet still felt the need to defend him. "He didn't. She died in childbirth."

Charlotte studied Violet's face carefully. "I cannot believe this. You care for him."

Unshed tears scalded the backs of Violet's eyelids, and she struggled to retain the tenuous hold she had on her composure. "I love him. I have loved him for a long time."

"And you never told me?"

Charlotte's mouth flattened, hurt lingering in her gaze, and Violet added guilt to the mountain of emotion dragging her down. "Forgive me. Things with Ravensthorpe progressed quickly, and he made it perfectly clear that it was temporary. That I was temporary—"

"That bastard." Charlotte stiffened, her fingers turning white on the walnut bedpost. "He seduced you and then refused to marry you."

"More like I seduced him, but yes."

"Even if you threw yourself at him, he should have told you no. I cannot believe he ruined you and then tossed you away!"

"That's not exactly what happened. Sit down and I'll tell you everything."

Stiffly, Charlotte moved to the bed and sat. Violet took a deep breath and launched into the entire tale, starting with watching Max with Lady Underhill and ending with the letter.

"Wait, he called you a *lark?*" Charlotte's brows went up, outrage clear in her tone. "We should storm into his house and put a bullet in his black heart."

That sounded a tad extreme. "He never lied to me. He never led me to believe it was more."

"You should hate him for how he treated you."

"I don't hate him." She swallowed and tried to keep her voice from shaking. "But while I still love him, I cannot be a secret. I deserve better."

"Indeed, you do." Charlotte reached forward and grasped Violet's hand. "So what will you do about his letter?"

"I haven't decided." She lifted the note with her free hand and tapped it against her thigh. "At best, it's an apology for telling my father. At worst, it's a formal ending to our . . . friendship."

"Do you think there is a chance he's come around on marriage?"

I won't marry you.

"No. Absolutely not." Time and time again Max had made this clear.

"There's always Sundridge. He's not so terrible."

Violet gave her friend a disbelieving look. "He's awful, Charlotte. I won't marry him."

"Then what will you do? You must marry, especially now."

Because Max had ruined her.

Violet didn't feel ruined, however. She felt tired and deeply sad. Fed up with both her parents and society. Ready to make her own decisions and escape any reminders of Max.

This was not the future she wanted, years of circling ballrooms and watching as Max ignored her. How long before he followed another woman out to the gardens? Perhaps he already had.

She pressed a fist into her stomach. Everything hurt and staying here wouldn't solve any of her problems. Her parents would only marry her off to some fop and Max would carry on with his paramours.

She didn't want that life—one that would tear her down, bit by bit, day after day until she was absolutely nothing at all. No, she wanted love and a large family, a place where she fit in, but on her terms, not with a man who cared only about her dowry.

It appeared she must find happiness all on her own.

"Violet, you're scaring me," Charlotte said when the silence stretched. "What can I do to help you?"

Plans began forming in Violet's mind, wisps of ideas that grew clearer, slowly revealing a path forward like an exposed image darkening in a developer bath. She could see it, a fate of her own choosing, even if the prospect seemed daunting at the moment.

Her heart pounded with renewed purpose and resolve. "Actually, there is something you may do. I need you to deliver a package for me."

* * *

MAX STUMBLED TOWARD THE CARRIAGE, his legs shaking like jelly. The dockside buildings dipped and swirled, the midmorning sun causing the world to look like a kaleidoscope. Somehow, he put one foot in front of the other and managed to reach his conveyance.

A groom rushed to assist him, but he held up a hand. He deserved the punishment. "No need," he mumbled. "Just allow me to get inside."

Once on the seat, he collapsed like a newborn foal and closed his eyes. He'd been rowing on the Thames for three hours, as he'd been doing every morning for the last fortnight. He hadn't rowed this much since Eton, and his body did not appreciate the punishment. There were blisters on his fingers and palms, his back screamed in pain, and he thought he might have cracked a rib.

But he would not stop. The torture was necessary.

Many times, he'd considered departing London. After all, he had three estates and several townhouses to choose from, including a beautiful apartment in Paris. Yet he couldn't bring himself to go. He couldn't bring himself to leave her behind.

You're a fool. She is better off without you.

He gasped when they bounced over a particularly nasty hole in the road, the agony in his side like being stabbed with a dull knife. Moaning, he clutched the leather seat and tried not to vomit on the carriage floor.

"Apologies, Your Grace!" the coachman called.

Several calming breaths later, the spots receded from his eyes. "Fuck," he whispered.

You cannot do this much longer.

There was no choice. He couldn't sleep at night and this was the only way to exhaust himself enough to rest. When he returned home, he'd fall into bed and finally find a few hours' sleep. It was a neat little system he'd worked out, one that was keeping him sane.

Last week, he'd broken down and written to her, stupidly confessing how much he missed her and apologizing for telling her father. He'd also asked to see her, certain that they could smooth over their troubles if given a chance.

She sent the unopened letter back.

And that wasn't all she returned. She also returned the photographs of him, the ones without his clothes. As if she couldn't stand to look at him. That had hurt worse than the unopened letter.

She must hate him—and he couldn't blame her.

So he rowed. When he wasn't on the river, he was brooding by the fire, draining every bottle of brandy in the cellar. He was pathetic, a miserable husk of a man, yet he couldn't seem to bring himself out of this funk. Nothing mattered. Work piled on his desk; food went uneaten.

He missed her desperately, like a piece of his soul had been removed. This was nothing like when he'd lost his first wife. Losing Violet was a howling despair haunting his every waking moment. He'd found happiness, had tasted salvation, and then let it slip away through his foolishness and vanity.

I hope you rot in hell, Ravensthorpe.

Indeed, he was already there.

Another carriage sat outside his home, but Max couldn't bother with callers at the moment. Or ever. "Send them away," he told his butler as he stumbled over the threshold.

"Your Grace," his butler said, following. "Lady Mayhew is here to see you and insisted on waiting."

Max froze. "Did you say . . . Lady Mayhew?"

"Indeed. She is in the front drawing room."

Why was Charles's wife here? They'd never liked one another. In the early days of her marriage, she had blamed Max for corrupting Charles. Out of loyalty to Charles, Max hadn't denied it, though Charles required no help whatsoever when it came to corruption.

Still, this visit might have something to do with Violet. "I'll see her now."

A horrified look crossed his butler's face—likely because Max wasn't bothering to change before receiving a caller—but Max didn't care. This might concern Violet, and that was far more important than the sorry state of his person offending Lady Mayhew.

He slowly made his way to the drawing room, doing his best not to crumple onto the Italian marble floor.

"Lady Mayhew. This is a surprise."

"Ravensthorpe. I have to say, you've looked better." She was perched on the edge of the sofa, appearing ready to bolt at a moment's notice. She and her daughter had the same hair, a similar chin and bone structure. It sent a fresh wave of agony through him just to look at her.

He cleared his throat. "What may I do for you this morning?"

"I've come to seek a favor."

"A favor from me?" This was unexpected.

She nodded once. "You see, when a wife is saddled with a lying, philandering husband, she must develop a trusted and reliable source of informants. These are often servants, which is certainly the case in my household. And I've recently been given an interesting piece of news."

"Oh?"

"According to Violet's maid, you wrote a letter to my daughter, which she returned along with some other papers. More letters, perhaps?"

Max braced himself, saying nothing and allowing her to come to the point.

"Regardless, my husband confirmed that you and Violet had been involved for some time."

"Our involvement has ended."

"I assumed as much, based on the returning of your note. Not to mention that she's disappeared."

He blinked. "What do you mean, disappeared?"

"She is missing. She left the morning after sending back your letter."

Max strangled the armrests in a death grip, his fingertips digging into the wood. That had been a week ago. Why hadn't he been—?

Fuck. Of course, he hadn't been informed. Charles didn't want him in the same room as his daughter.

Max had to find her. He would tear this city apart with his bare hands, if necessary. A hundred terrible things could befall a sweet young woman such as Violet in this god-awful city. "I assume the police have been summoned and are currently searching for her."

"No. My husband thought it best if we kept this quiet. Family only, that sort of thing." She studied his face. "But it's plain you still care for her."

"I do." He swallowed, his chest pulling tight. "I beg your pardon, but I didn't plan for it to happen."

"You needn't apologize to me. In fact, this makes things easier."

He bounced his leg, anxious for the woman to take her leave so that he could begin searching for Violet. He had to make sure she was safe. "Easier, how?"

"I need her married, Ravensthorpe. As quickly as possible."

His lips twisted derisively. "Yes, she was aware. Hardly matters to whom, does it?"

"You judge me, of course. As a man, you wouldn't understand that all women are pushed into marriage, whether we want it or not. We are traded like cattle, treated little better than dirt."

"Yet you treat your daughter the same."

"Violet is smart. Independent. A thoroughly likable girl. I love her, I do —but I have put up with Charles for long enough. It's time to be free."

Max sat up sharply, ignoring the pain in his side. "Free? Are you saying . . .?"

"I plan to divorce him as soon as Violet is married. The solicitor is ready with the paperwork."

"Divorce?"

She gave him a brittle smile. "I am tired of being disrespected and lied to. You, perhaps better than most, understand what I've endured for the last twenty years. He's fathered two bastards that I know of, probably more. I won't allow him in my bed any longer. Do you want to know why?"

Max remained silent, almost dreading the answer.

She continued, "My husband is riddled with disease. He's had mercury treatments to try and cure it. Lord knows it would be a miracle if I were not infected as well. I cannot stand to look at him any longer. If I must endure the scandal of a divorce to be free of that man, then so be it."

The explanation made sense. If Violet had known, it would have eased her mind regarding her mother's motives. His heart ached for his little mouse. "You should tell your daughter. She believes you want rid of her."

"And I am sorry for that. When I have the chance, I will explain it to her. I had thought to wait until she was married, when she would better understand what happens in the marital bed." She cocked a brow. "But I see you've taken care of that."

"I . . ." For once, Max was at a loss for words. He had taken Violet's innocence against his better judgment.

"Go and find her, Ravensthorpe. Use your considerable influence to locate my daughter and convince her to forgive you. Then marry her, quickly. You, more than most, are immune from any scandal. Your name will shelter her from any . . . unpleasantness during the divorce proceedings."

Marry?

He hadn't wished to marry again, yet he was miserable without her. He couldn't let her go—he needed Violet in his life, in his bed. In his home, making him smile and taking photographs. Being with her was easy, fulfilling in a way he hadn't experienced with any other woman before.

Could he try again? He'd failed with Rebecca, but Violet was nothing like his late wife. Violet was a spark of optimism and light, a beacon of joy and happiness. Intelligent and lusty, she would never bore him or let him run roughshod over her. Moreover, he was different than the selfish man of twenty-five, who'd believed himself invincible. He would treat Violet as a wife should be treated.

Violet . . . *his wife*. He liked the sound of that. Quite a lot, actually.

Suddenly, he didn't care whether Charles disapproved or whether people sneered at the age difference. He had to have her. To love and hold her until he took his last breath.

He tapped his fingertips against his thigh. She had disappeared, but Max would find her. In fact, he had an inkling of where she might have gone. "I cannot promise she'll forgive me, but I will try."

"Good," Lady Mayhew said, rising. "She is headstrong, but Violet's been in love with you for years."

Her mother had noticed when Max hadn't? Of course, he'd been busy avoiding Violet since her debut, terrified of his feelings for her. That ended now. He was ready to admit he loved her and that he couldn't live without her.

He stood. "I am not the only one who must seek Violet's forgiveness. You've hurt her, you know."

She winced, her brow furrowed. "That was not my intention, but I suppose I have been so focused on my own happiness that I forgot about Violet's. I haven't been the best mother."

"Help her understand. Be there for her."

Lady Mayhew cocked her head, her lips pursed in thoughtfulness. "You really care for her, don't you?"

"More than anything else in the world."

"Make her happy, Ravensthorpe."

Resolve settled in his chest like a rock, and he nodded. "You may count on it, my lady."

CHAPTER 11

*V*iolet poured hot water into the teapot and returned the kettle to the tiny stove. Then she placed the lid on the pot to allow the leaves to steep. The stove had been a challenge, but she'd grown proficient with it in the past week.

Heartache turned a person productive, it seemed.

Since leaving home, she'd taken photos and explored the city. Walked the streets and observed the inhabitants. She'd also met her new neighbors, three other young women living in apartments above the camera shop in Chelsea. The girls worked in department stores and offices, each a new kind of independent woman, one in control of her own life. Just like Violet.

She hadn't told them of her aristocratic upbringing, but they knew. It was in the way she spoke, the way she dressed. Even in the tea she drank, apparently. But they didn't judge her. Instead, they fondly called her "countess," which Violet didn't mind. She'd never had a nickname before.

Actually, she'd never had this many friends before, either.

She still missed Max, though. He was in her head, her heart . . . in her bones. Part of her regretted not reading his letter, but it wouldn't have said what she wished to hear. Max would never tell her sweet words of undying devotion, the things a husband said to a wife. After all, she was a lark to him. A woman to pass the time.

Goodness, that still hurt.

Pouring her tea, she gave thanks that at least she hadn't conceived a baby. That was one worry she needn't add to the pile, which now included finding employment to cover her rent and living expenses. And those particular problems grew more pressing by the day as her funds dwindled.

Had he thought about her at all? Or had he picked up with one of his many mistresses?

A knock sounded on her door. She placed her cup in the saucer and stood, smoothing her dress. It was probably one of her friends stopping by to have a chat.

Opening the door, she jerked in surprise.

The Duke of Ravensthorpe stood there. Max. Here. In Chelsea. How . . .?

Oh, yes. She'd once told him about her camera shop idea. How had he remembered?

Dark blue eyes burned from under the rim of his hat, his mouth set in a firm, determined line. Though his face was gaunt, he was unmistakably a duke, with his frame draped in expensive fabrics and the gold of his watch fob glinting in the daylight. She could hardly breathe due to the need to throw herself at him.

No, no more playing the fool.

Her friend Irene stood next to him. "I hope it's all right that I let him in. He said he knew you." Irene leaned in. "Is he really a duke?"

"It's fine, Irene. Thank you." Drawing in a deep breath, she said, "Would Your Grace care to come in?"

Max removed his bowler and stepped into her tiny apartment. Irene's eyes were as big as saucers when Violet whispered, "I'll tell you later," and shut the door.

He dominated the small room, a force of nature in her private space. Violet wasn't certain where to go or what to do. Why was he here?

He held his hat and cane in gloved hands and inspected his surroundings. No doubt he found it lacking, but Violet certainly wouldn't apologize for where she lived. She loved this place.

Without prompting, she produced another cup and saucer, set it on the table, and poured tea for him. Then she retook her seat and calmly sipped her tea, waiting for him to break the silence.

After clearing his throat, he sat and removed his gloves. "Are you curious as to how I located you?" His voice was rough and cracked, like he hadn't used it in days.

"I once mentioned that I would rent a small apartment above a camera shop in Chelsea."

"Yes, and fortunate for me, there are just two camera shops in Chelsea, and this is the only one with apartments atop it."

She frowned, her brows lowering. "Why is that fortunate?"

"Because I needed to find you."

"Interested in a lark, were you?"

He winced. "I saw you leave with your father so it's obvious you overheard us, and I'm sorry I ever said anything as stupid as that. I didn't mean it."

"Why? It's true. That's all we were to one another."

"No, that wasn't all, not for me."

Bitterness welled up in her chest like a fog, its dismal fingers sinking into her heart to squeeze. "Forgive me if I have a hard time believing that, Max."

"Violet, I was trying to convince myself there was nothing between us. That I could go on living without you after you'd happily married your Sundridge or Wingfield. But I cannot do it. I am utterly miserable without you."

Hope fluttered in her stomach, but she beat it back with a ruthlessness that hadn't existed two weeks ago. "Because you need someone in your bed."

"Because I need *you* in my bed. In my life. With me, wherever I go. For however long I have left on this earth."

Her hands curled into fists, her skin burning with humiliation and anger. The gall of this man. "I see. You found me living here and assumed I would jump at the chance to become your mistress or whatever else you wanted. That I would be content to stay hidden and wait for your scraps. Well, you may return to Mayfair and shove that cane—"

"Wait." He reached into his coat pocket and produced a square box, which he sat on the tabletop. "I came here to ask you to be my wife."

The room spun, and Violet's mouth fell open. Was that . . .? No, it couldn't be. "But you said . . ."

"I know what I said, but that was before I tried to row myself to death in the Thames."

She shook her head, confused. "What?"

"Never mind. What's important is that I do not wish to exist in a world without you calling me 'Your Grace' in that breathy way of yours, or running your fingers through my hair. Or taking photographs of me, or talking of philosophy and history and all the other clever things in your head. I cannot do it. I need you."

"You want to marry me? Marry? Me?"

He sighed in that arrogant way of his, as if he hated repeating himself. The sound was so Ravensthorpe that she nearly grinned. "Yes, Violet. Please, marry me."

She bit her lip, not quite ready to give in, though her heart was nearly bursting with happiness. "I thought you were too old for me."

"I only care what you think. Do you think I am too old for you?"

"Of course not. What about my father?"

"I believe he'll soon be too busy with other matters to worry about us."

"Whatever does that mean?"

"Your mother came to see me. She plans to begin divorce proceedings. She was merely waiting until you were married off."

Divorce? Violet stared at the wall, her mind whirling. "Was that why she was so eager to see me settled?"

"Yes."

She paused, uncertain how to feel about this revelation. Looking back, the fights with Papa and the emotional distance from the family made a bit more sense. Mama clearly hadn't been happy, not for years, so if she needed to divorce Papa for her well-being then Violet would support the decision.

Yet why had Mama pushed for Violet to make an unhappy match, as well? If anyone knew the risks of marriage, it was her mother.

Mama should have tried to protect her, not sacrifice Violet for her own gain. Instead, her mother had washed her hands of Violet's future, practically pushing her out the door to any man who'd have her.

And why had Mama shared this information with Max, instead of her daughter?

Suspicion cast a shadow over the moment, and her stomach churned with emotion. "So this," she said, indicating the square box, "is your way of helping her?"

"No." Dipping elegantly onto one knee, he took out the ring and held it up in his fingers. "This is my way of keeping you all for myself. I'll never deserve you, not today. Not tomorrow. Never. You're beautiful and pure and I am the very Devil. But I love you, Violet Littleton, and I shall do absolutely everything in my power to ensure you never forget it, not for a moment."

She covered her mouth, her heart skipping in her chest. "You love me?"

"Indeed, in the very worst way."

She stared at his gold collar stud and voiced her deepest fear. "You won't hide me away? I'll be your wife in every sense of the word?"

With one finger, he lifted her chin to meet her gaze. A wrinkle had formed between his brows. "I'd be proud to have you by my side. I need you. Without you, I'm wrecked. You hold all my happiness in your dainty, camera-loving hands."

"I am not that powerful. After all, even you call me 'little mouse.'"

He stroked her jaw with the backs of his knuckles. "Violet, do you not remember the fable of the mouse and the lion? It is the mouse who shows great courage and bravery, saving the lion from a slow, painful death."

Oh, goodness. She hadn't considered that. Her belly dipped and swooped, as if she might actually swoon. "Are you saying I saved you?"

"Of course, you have, darling girl. You brought color and joy to a man who had lived in gray for so very long." He leaned in and pressed his forehead to hers. "You are the sunshine to my bleary dark soul."

"Max . . ."

"Is that a yes?"

Taking a deep breath, she steeled her voice into something more businesslike. "I have conditions."

The side of his mouth hitched, his expression soft as he rose to his full height. "Is that so?"

"I wish to keep this apartment. That way, I'll have a place just for me when I need to get away."

A muscle jumped his jaw, his dark gaze sparking as he studied her. "Is this about having a lover on the side? I won't share you, Violet. Not with anyone."

"I do not want another lover." She thought of his first wife. "And if we marry, I won't share you either."

"Agreed."

"That easily? Forgive my skepticism, considering your proclivity for lascivious behavior. Does the Duke of Ravensthorpe possess the ability for monogamy?"

"He does, if the woman in his life is you, with your clever brain and bold spirit. If you need to keep the apartment to retain a bit of your independence, then I'll not complain."

"Independence—and my photography. I'll use it as a portrait studio."

"As long as said portraits involve clothing."

She stood and closed the distance between them, using a fingertip to trace the edge of his collar. Goose bumps appeared on his skin and she smiled up at him. "You are the only one allowed to pose for my nude portraits, Your Grace."

A growl rumbled deep in his chest. "Yes to the apartment. What else?"

"I want to try for children."

His large body tensed. "No, Violet. I could not bear it if—"

"I am not your first wife." She stroked his lapel, soothing him. "I'll be fine. But I want a piece of you and a piece of me to live on, together, to make this world a better place."

"Goddamn it," he said and shifted his gaze to the wall. "What if you die?"

"Death stalks us every day. I could choke on a fishbone at dinner and die. But I've spent my entire life watching, observing, never fitting in while waiting for something to happen, and I am tired of waiting. I want excitement and laughter, little feet running through the halls. Most of all, I want to see your face in our children."

"Christ, Violet." He bent to kiss her hard on the lips. "I suppose I'll need to find the best doctors in this bloody country to watch over you, then."

"Does that mean you agree to my conditions?"

"I don't have a choice, do I? I will give you anything you want to get my ring on your finger."

She nearly swayed, the exhilaration almost too much to bear. "Anything I want? Oh, the heady power of having the Duke of Ravensthorpe at my feet."

"As long as you never leave me, I'll lie at your feet anytime you like."

The afternoon light played across the angles of his face and throat. Harsh and beautiful, he was hers, and she'd never tire of looking at him. "What about now? I like the idea of more nude portraits of you."

Taking her hand, he slipped his ring onto her finger. Then he reached into his coat pocket and withdrew a folded stack of photographs. She cocked her head. "Are those the pictures I took of you?"

"I thought I should return them to their rightful owner." When she moved to take them, he lifted the stack far above her head. "With one condition."

Crafty man. Of course he had his own condition. "Which is?"

"That you use them for their intended purpose while I watch."

He wanted her to do *that* in front of him? "Now?"

"Right now." His gaze burned with adoration and desire, but there was something else there, as well. Something new that was serious and far more meaningful.

He loves me.

Her skin could barely contain the joy coursing through her. Sliding her arms around his neck, she pulled him closer and put her lips near his ear. "Yes, Your Grace."

The End.

* * *

Want more of Joanna's sinfully sexy heroes set in Gilded Age New York City?

Check out The Devil of Downtown!

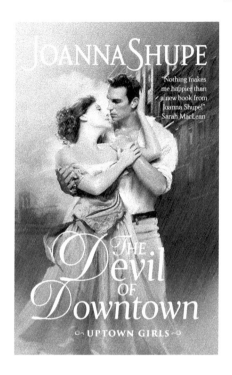

Manhattan kingpin.
Brilliant mastermind.
Gentleman gangster.

He's built a wall around his heart...

Orphaned and abandoned on the Bowery's mean streets, Jack Mulligan survived on strength, cunning, and ambition. Now he rules his territory better than any politician or copper ever could. He didn't get here by being soft. But in uptown do-gooder Justine Greene—the very definition of an iron fist in a velvet glove—Jack may have met his match.

She wears hers on her sleeve...

Justine is devoted to tracking down deadbeat husbands and fighting for fair working conditions. When her mission brings her face-to-face with Jack, she's shocked to find the man behind the criminal empire is considerably more charming and honorable than many "gentlemen" she knows.

Forming an unlikely alliance, they discover an unexpected desire. And when Justine's past catches up with them, Jack may be her only hope of survival. Is she ready to make a deal with the devil?

Start reading The Devil of Downtown, book #3 in Joanna's acclaimed Uptown Girls series from Avon/HarperCollins.

A NOTE FROM THE AUTHOR

I hope you enjoyed this short sexy story about Max and Violet. I had a blast writing it.

Thanks to the lighter, more portable, affordable cameras produced in the late 19th-century, "Kodak Girls" became a Victorian/Gilded Age phenomenon. Photography was very popular, including scandalous nudes, many of which can still be seen today.

Also popular in the late 19th-century were nipple rings. Mostly in Paris, but also with the English aristocracy. And both women and men had this done, just like today. Violet definitely would have gone to Paris and had her nipples pierced as a surprise for Max . . .

If you like these historical tidbits and want more, sign up for my Gilded News newsletter. You'll also get book news, sneak peeks, reading recommendations, historical fashion plates, and more!

MORE BY JOANNA SHUPE

The Fifth Avenue Rebels:

The Heiress Hunt

The Lady Gets Lucky

The Bride Goes Rogue

The Uptown Girls:

The Rogue of Fifth Avenue

The Prince of Broadway

The Devil of Downtown

The Four Hundred Series:

A Daring Arrangement

A Scandalous Deal

A Notorious Vow

The Knickerbocker Club:

Tycoon

Magnate

Baron

Mogul

Wicked Deceptions:

The Courtesan Duchess

The Harlot Countess

The Lady Hellion

Novellas:

How The Dukes Stole Christmas Anthology

Miracle on Ladies' Mile

ABOUT THE AUTHOR

USA Today Bestselling author **Joanna Shupe** has always loved history, ever since she saw her first Schoolhouse Rock cartoon. Since 2015, her books have appeared on numerous yearly "best of" lists, including Publishers Weekly, *The Washington Post*, Kirkus Reviews, Kobo, and BookPage.

Sign up for Joanna's Gilded News newsletter for book news, sneak peeks, reading recommendations, historical tidbits, and more!

www.joannashupe.com

Printed in the USA
CPSIA information can be obtained
at www.ICGtesting.com
LVHW010414021024
792705LV00018B/1105